GABRIEL LANCE
AND THE CURSED ONES

A Fairy Tale by:

Karla J.M. Brading

KARLA J.M. BRADING

**Also by Karla J.M. Brading
for young adults:**

Destiny in Blood

Blood of Angels

Dark Blood Falling

Whispers of a Reaper

Eyes Like Death

For Children:

That Quiet Place

The Zombie Jig and Jive
and Other Creepy Tales

KARLA J.M. BRADING

Copyright@Karla J.M. Brading

First Published in 2012 by
Karla J.M. Brading Publishing

1

All characters in this publication are fictitious and any
resemblance to real persons, living or dead, is purely
coincidental.

ISBN 978-0-9561007-2-6

Printed and bound in Britain by
Print Evolution

Cover Photography: Kitty KEMS Photography
Model: Stephanie K Davenport

For Millie

KARLA J.M. BRADING

Everyone deserves a happily ever after...right?

KARLA J.M. BRADING

GABRIEL LANCE
AND THE CURSED ONES

Chapter 1

There was once a boy called Gabriel Lance, who never slept – not even when a warm fire blazed in the heath, or a feather pillow met his cold cheek.

His skin was as white as the frosting on the tallest of mountains and his eyes, big and blue, were pale and wonderful like a wolves. The jagged cut of his midnight hair fell like daggers about his sharp, cheekbones and when he walked, head bent low to the ground; his fringe always shielded most of his handsome face. This he did intentionally, so that the townsfolk would not recognise him. He kept to himself *always* and never uttered his full name to a living soul.

Gabriel never slept because he was already dead. His body functioned on the blood of others, which gave him the strength to keep moving. It was a sad truth that Gabriel's soul had detached itself from his physical state a long time ago, departing for an unknown realm – a realm he hoped was keeping it safe. And so he wandered restlessly between towns, carrying emptiness in his heart.

But this story starts with a library. An old library with many stone steps leading to a great pair of oak doors, which Gabriel stood quietly in awe of. It was the eve of his Death-Day – a name he had chosen to mark the date of his life's end – and it was at this particular library in the great town of Wallace that Gabriel had lost everything.

"You're so morbid," whispered a voice in the night.

He pulled a simple hair clip from his trouser pocket and fumbled with the lock, ignoring the ghost-girl at his shoulder.

Annabel was a spirit and an irritating one at that. Many years previous, when Gabriel had been bent on his hands and knees, wracked with pain and an overpowering thirst for blood, he had taken her life. He did not kill very often. It had to be in very special circumstances – or if in his fury, he had no choice but to fight back – that he risk taking the life of a human; especially one so young. But she had been alone in the twilight, perched on a swing, having chosen this particular night to run away from home.

When Annabel's spirit had separated from her flesh, she had felt compelled to follow Gabriel everywhere he went. Too much distance between them caused her pain and it was only when they were reunited, that Annabel realised she could not leave Gabriel's side. Ever.

Gabriel, unsure why he was haunted by just *one* of the souls he'd destroyed, had taken it upon himself to speak with an old gypsy woman, who had been blind in both eyes. With wrinkled hands the colour of mud, she had touched his cool flesh and asked him about the object he had stolen from the young girl's body. Around Annabel's little white neck, there had once hung a beautiful gold pendant, with a dazzling red jewel in the shape of a heart. It had been a gift from her grandmother, to wear on her first day of school. But Gabriel had snapped it from about her throat as he had drained her of blood and according to the wise gypsy; this act had bound Annabel to him, for all eternity, lest he return the necklace to her grave.

If Gabriel had known that pocketing the jewellery of the dead would cause him such a burden, he would never have done so. But he had learned the hard way, like most do in life. His reasons for taking it in the first place had been plain: he needed to remind himself of the evil deed he had committed, so that he might find other means of getting blood than killing little girls. Needless to say, with Annabel floating mere inches from him on a daily basis, he hadn't killed another little girl since.

"You're going to get caught, you know?" she complained, crossing her skinny, translucent arms over the front of her white school blouse. Her blonde pigtails floated and bobbed around her pretty face.

The lock clicked and fell to the floor with a *thunk*.

"The hunters might mistake you for a Nightcrawler and put a bullet in your back."

Nightcrawler's are ghastly creatures. When a vampire is starved of blood over a long period of time, their faces and body parts melt and distort in a horrific manner. Elbows and knees buckle in odd directions and limbs twist unnaturally. Most Nightcrawler's scour the floors with the use of their knuckles, not unlike a gorilla, galumphing along in packs of twos and threes. They live on the outskirts of towns and in the midst of starvation, forget the language of humans. With clicks and howls, they communicate to one another, eating any living creature that gets too close. All towns have hunters on duty when darkness falls, just in case a Nightcrawler develops the courage to venture deeper into town.

"You insult me," Gabriel replied, in words so soft not even the sharpest of ears could pick them up. Annabel, however, was hovering so close to his face, she could happily read his lips. "I'm not *nearly* that ugly."

"No, you're right. You're not. I reckon you're *uglier*." She tittered to herself, squeezing between the gap in the oak doors, before Gabriel even had a chance to set foot amidst the shadows within.

"Come on, slow poke!" she howled, voice echoing off the grey, stone walls. Annabel, loud and uncaring as she was, could only be heard by Gabriel. She could shout and bawl and scream in the faces of others and no one but he would bat an eyelid. He was glad of it though. He did not wish the girl's pestering and banter on anyone.

Gabriel slipped inside, coat tails fluttering in the breeze that his inhuman speed generated. Annabel was lying on a bookcase, shooing a spider away with her ghostly paws. She wafted the fat arachnid from its perch, which landed on Gabriel's shoulder as he passed.

"Annabel," he breathed, curling his hand around the eight legged intruder. He propped it against the spine of an old book, where it scuttled away in distress.

"You know I'll leave you alone when you put my pendant back," she retorted, head dangling from the bookcase as she hung upside down.

"I'm getting there, alright," he hissed. The ghost was testing his patience. He was here for peace of mind… to remember who he was. Not to discuss the same pressing matters they went over and over, again and again.

"Slow poke, that's what you are! My Granny moves faster than you and she died a hundred years ago."

"*You* died a hundred years ago," he reminded her.

"Oh, has it been that long?" she wondered, brushing her fingers along the spines of dusty books as she shadowed him.

"Longer," he mumbled.

"You're getting old too, Gabriel. Even though you look like a cute, ickle fifteen year old."

He didn't answer.

"Maybe this was the town I lived in…before you killed me?"

"No."

"It could be!"

"It's not. This was the town *I* lived in before *I* died. I told you this already."

"I thought we were looking for *my* town?"

"We are." He gritted his teeth.

"I think it's silly that you forgot where I came from."

"It was a *long* time ago and I was new to this. They chased me out when they found your body. I almost died. *Again*."

"A hundred years is a long time, Gabriel. My grave could have vanished by now."

"We can only hope that's not the case," he said,

with a hint of sarcasm.

He bent down and stroked the flagstone floor. They were the same stones he'd fallen upon when the dark figure – that now haunted his nightmares – had appeared as if from mist and bitten down on his neck. He remembered how he violently thrashed, trying to knock the attacker to the ground, but they had been far too strong for his weak arms. And once he'd been bitten he had watched that person, or thing, walk away as if it had all meant nothing, words frozen on his blue lips. In such a vast library, it had been hours before anyone had even noticed he was hurt.

"Are you listening to me?"

"No."

"You always think about yourself."

"If that were the case, I wouldn't be retracing my steps for you, now would I?"

She wrinkled her little, upturned nose. "Is it because you love me, Gabriel?"

"It's because you *annoy* me, Annabel."

He remembered how death had come slowly to him. His eyes had closed and then re-opened again. His heart had painfully ceased its primal function and his body became numbingly cold. And his hunger, well, his hunger intensified beyond all measure.

So the question on Gabriel's lips was: why him?

Chapter 2

"Why did you bring me here?"

Gabriel rose from his crouched position and met the doleful eyes of his companion. Annabel was bobbing up and down on a draught that was sweeping along the aisles from the open front doors. They could hear the wind complaining against the windows. It would no doubt be a fierce and stormy night, likely to last long after dawn broke.

"I thought it would help me remember a face-"

"And did it?" she pressed.

He shook his head, black hair sweeping over his eyes as he looked down once more. "I remember nothing but the dark cape of some fiend, as they left me to die."

"That's sad," she sympathised, whilst circling him. "That's really sad – not knowing who killed you."

Gabriel reached a hand inside his coat and pulled out a gold plated pocket watch. It was a family heirloom – a gift handed down to him when his father had developed an incurable flu, which had eventually taken his life. The watch told Gabriel that the midnight hour had already slipped him by. They had lingered long enough.

"If it makes you feel better, Gabriel, I want you to

know I'm glad you showed me your face when you did it. When you killed me, I mean."

"What an odd thing for a person to say," he replied, realising only too late that Annabel was less of a 'person' and more of a - well - a spiritual pain in his behind.

He tucked his watch away and strode along the flagstones in the direction of the open doors. Annabel swooped along behind him, arms folded behind her head. She was riding the currents as if they were ocean waves.

"You just looked so sad," she said, "when you came for me on the swings. Your eyes were full of sadness and your face, so full of pain."

Gabriel disliked conjuring images of the little girl's death, but did not have the heart to demand silence from her. She was dead. It was his fault. She had every right to be annoyed with him.

"I never meant to –"

"I know you didn't," she cut in. "Something would have probably got me in the end, anyway. Our town was full of wild dogs and they could get pretty nasty."

Gabriel stopped. "What else?" he asked.

Annabel paused, level with the vampire's enchanting blue eyes.

"When the bus took us home from school, they used to bite at the tires. It used to scare me. I thought they'd chew right through and that they'd get on somehow—"

"What was the name of your school, Annabel?"

She was remembering her own town, for the first

time in many years. Never had she spoken of home, or mentioned how life had been when she was alive. All her empty head had ever told him was that she had run away from her parents – for reasons unknown – and that he had killed her in a playground.

"School...school." She wiggled her fingers against her pasty chin in deep thought. "Nope. Gone."

Gabriel rolled his eyes, just as a loud shot sounded in the night.

He looked down as a patch of blood bloomed over his stomach.

"*Gabriel?*" Annabel's eyes filled with panic. She tried mopping desperately at his wound, but the whites of her small, translucent hands disappeared inside his body in a useless fashion.

He ducked and scrambled for cover behind the main desk at the entrance. With his head propped against a shelf of books labelled *reserved*, he struggled with his shirt buttons. He needed to act quickly, or else his skin would heal with the bullet still inside.

"There are men outside. Hunters with guns!" Annabel reported, her face entirely poking through the wood of one door so that it appeared she were headless.

Gabriel ignored her. His fingers pried and found the hole in which the bullet had entered his flesh. With a wiggle and pinch, he plucked it from the weeping wound and tossed it onto the floor. And as he eyed it with relief, something else stirred in the peripherals of his vision.

Beyond the counter, directly opposite him, a shadow of a figure moved with an unnatural swagger.

"Nightcrawler," Annabel hissed. She spoke

quietly, though no one but Gabriel could hear her words. "It must be what they're hunting. Probably followed us in!"

Gabriel reached inside his coat and pulled out a cold, silver blade, the length of his forearm. The Nightcrawler had paused to smell the air, turning its head sharply this way and that.

"What's it doing?" Annabel squeaked. She was too afraid to go near it, though it would not have sensed her presence. The Nightcrawler's relentless clicking in the back of its throat and its mangled visage made Annabel's bones turn in their grave, (wherever it may be!). It was hunched over – a huge lump protruding from its spine. In the moonlight pooling over the front desk from the grimy windows, they could make out its misshapen skull and heard the slapping of saliva as it drooled thickly from its parted lips.

If there had been no hunters to speak of, in such close proximity, Gabriel would have sprung from his hiding place – wounded or not – and stabbed the vicious parasite with his blade. A slice to its heart would surely end it. But he feared another bullet wound.

The sound of doors being kicked open by heavy boots left him paralysed.

"Back up!" screamed a man. He was in a long brown coat that whipped about his legs in the wind that blustered from behind him. Upon his head, a cowboy hat perched.

"There you are –"

The Nightcrawler clicked more loudly and jumped onto the counter. Its legs were longer than a human's and its thighs were incredibly thick in circumference.

A second shot was fired off.

Gabriel placed his hands over his ears and ducked lower. The cowboy was so intent on the hunt that he hadn't noticed the vampire boy cowering nearby, armed and bloody.

"Back up! Where are you?!"

The doors swung open once more to reveal two teenage boys, panting and brandishing crossbows. In the shadows of the darkened library, it was hard to discern their features, but if their posture and height were anything to go by, Gabriel would have believed them identical.

"Shoot it, for crying out loud!"

An arrow sliced through the air and Annabel let out a roar of surprise as it passed through her forehead and into the back of the leaping Nightcrawler.

"Make it stop, Gabriel! Make it stop!" she begged.

Gabriel shifted his arm, gripping onto a ledge. In that moment, a crossbow was aimed at him from above.

"What about this one, Pa'?"

The man fired his shotgun and the Nightcrawler fell to the flagstones with a *splat*. "Bulls-eye!" he celebrated, waving his gun in the air.

Gabriel scowled up at the silhouette that was plaguing him. Annabel buried her head in his chest, searching for comfort he could not physically give.

"What was that, boy?" the man called.

The boy signalled with his crossbow. The man

and the other boy joined his side.

"What have we here then? A thief?" the cowboy said. "Jason, find me a light switch. I can't see a thing in this darkness."

There was a shuffling of feet as one of the boys left hastily, on his quest to bring light to the dismal confines of the room. Gabriel remained frozen in place when the surrounding area lit up at last, and he took it upon himself to mimic the action of breathing. It was a wise thing to do and had saved him twice in the past.

"Why are you in here?" the man demanded.

"I saw the creature and I was scared," he replied, feigning terror.

The man frowned. "So you found the time to break in, for *safety*?"

Gabriel nodded.

Annabel was on her feet, fists all balled up. She pummelled the man's chest and yelled, "Let us leave, you brute! We've got more important things to do!"

But Gabriel's focus remained on the eyes of his interrogator. "I have quick hands."

The man didn't look convinced. "But not quick legs, I take it?"

"Not quick enough, no," he lied.

"And you didn't think to close the door behind you -?"

"No, Sir. I wasn't thinking straight."

The man scratched the stubble on his chin. "Why didn't you ring the bell?"

It was only when the man lifted his head to the giant bell that hovered nearby that this particular bronze implement became apparent to the vampire. It hadn't been a part of the fixtures and fittings when Gabriel had been human, that was for sure. But then again, Nightcrawler's had been unheard of back then too.

"You're lying to me. Everyone in this town knows; you see a monster, you ring the bell. Then someone with a gun comes running."

So every building had a bell. He'd overlooked this fact. Next time, he would be sure to do his research before entering a town.

"Is that blood?" asked one of the young hunters. Gabriel could see now that the boys were in fact twins; hair the colour of copper pennies and eyes an interesting shade of green.

"Blood?" the man repeated.

Panicked, Gabriel summoned all his energy and with great speed and agility, he vaulted over the counter and belted through the oak doors.

Clang!

His skull exploded with pain. Stars spiralled across his vision.

Annabel floated to the step as he crumpled to the floor. Terror seeped from her ghostly chest – he could sense it.

"Oh Gabriel!" she shrieked and shot a look of pure anger at an old man leaning against the wall with a shovel in his hand. He lit a cigarette, his eyes hidden beneath the rim of a cowboy hat – this one sporting a bronze Sheriff's badge.

"Got you, blood sucker."

Chapter 3

Gabriel awoke in a darkened cell to the sound of ghostly crying. Annabel was on the grimy floor beside him, nestled in the curve of his body. Her narrow shoulders trembled and her colourless frame disappeared slightly beneath his chest as she quaked.

Gabriel raised a hand to the moonlight pouring through the rusty bars of a tiny window, too high to see out of even if he stood on tip toes. The movement of his fingertips through the illuminated dust particles stirred Annabel from her sorrow.

"Oh! You're awake –" She wiped her nose in the crook of her arm and turned to face the vampire.

Gabriel shifted into a seated position, his back resting against the damp stone wall. He placed one hand on each thigh and sighed, "Just about."

"I thought he'd knocked you senseless. I thought you'd never wake up and that I'd be stuck in this smelly cell with you forever."

He wiped a piece of muck from his trouser leg. "Are we close to the outskirts?"

She levitated and wrapped her little ghost-fingers around the bars of the tiny window; a spider's web rippling lazily as her nose went through it. "I see a church. And houses. Oh, and a pub! There's a man outside wobbling this way and that on the porch. He's got his arms around a lady."

"They keep their prisoners close to home then."

Opposite his cell was the grey shadow of another wall. He could hear nothing beyond it, even when he closed his eyes and honed his senses.

Annabel floated to the ground and began pacing. "What are you going to do?"

"We wait."

"I hate waiting!"

"You hate everything."

"No I don't!" She stamped her foot with a *squelch*. Gabriel was sure animals had been kept in this place at some point. The urine aroma wasn't human. It smelt of dog.

His stomach rumbled. Annabel's eyes met his. It was too much to hope that the men had left his vial of pig's blood in the pocket of his coat.

"They took it," the ghost explained, knowing only too well what he was after. "They took everything. Your dad's watch. Even my pendant."

His eyes flared with anger.

"I'm sorry I couldn't stop them for you, Gabriel —"

"It's no ones fault but my own." He waved his hand dismissively. "Go and take a look around for me. Tell me how many men linger here."

She nodded and left. In her absence, he approached the bars that prevented him from leaving his enclosure. They were iron made and coated in silver;

silver being a *real* problem as it made him weak if he was near it too long. Clearly, the town's folk had done their research on the undead.

When Annabel returned, she bore a wrinkled brow. "There's no one. This place is a graveyard. It gives me the creeps. Can't you break the bars and be done with it?"

"They've thought about that." He tapped a bar with his shoe. *Cluuuuung.* "Silver."

"So that's it then? They've left you here to die of starvation and I have to lie in whatever hole they eventually drop you into, haunting the bones of a boy who got caught by a cowboy, two ginger nit-wits and an old man with nose hair longer than my pigtails?!"

"Shh," Gabriel hissed. His ears detected movement.

Annabel *humphed* and bobbed up and down, her toes an inch from the dirty floor. Through her body, Gabriel watched the wall darken to pitch. A figure, tall and hooded, suddenly occupied the space before him. Its cloak was made of the blackest smoke; its silky tendrils feeding lazily through the bars to reach for him. Gabriel flinched as a finger of this alarming, black magic touched his cheek.

"You look like you've seen a –" Annabel turned and swallowed her own tongue.

The figure – with nothing but a sharp, white chin visible in the kiss of moonlight – reached out a bony hand. Its white index finger touched six bars. They turned to dust, and were no more.

"Come," came the whisper of a voice in Gabriel's

head, making his shrivelled, lifeless heart spasm unnaturally. "Go while the night still blankets this town and while the men fill their bellies with liquor."

Annabel scooted behind Gabriel's back in fear.

"You -" he said, but broke off.

The black, smoky tendrils clawed their way further into the room, scraping at the walls and filling the cell with its energy. Gabriel felt the prickle of electricity at the nape of his neck as the figure took three steps forward, its stride long and inhuman.

"Do you remember me?" Its cold, bony hand lifted once more and traced the line of Gabriel's jaw. "Do you dare to remember?"

His body remained frozen – a spell perhaps? – but his lips moved. "Yes."

A chuckle came from deep within the hood. The bony white fingers lifted, lightly pinching the hood's rim. Slowly, the figure pushed it back, revealing a white head with not a single hair upon it. Its eyes were jet in colour, glistening with what appeared to be an infinity of stars. Its nose was long and thin and its lips, non-existent. It was as if someone had slit a neat hole above its chin for the words to trickle out.

"I was a woman once." The figure grabbed Gabriel's face in its hands. "Not even I know what I am now."

His eyes widened in astonishment as his skin sizzled beneath its cold grasp.

"I am nothing. I am death itself."

Annabel had been quiet, up until now. "Let go of him, you witch!"

A milky hand shot out and grabbed her by the chin. Not only could the strange figure see and hear Annabel, but they could touch her too; as if she were a physical entity.

"You will respect me *child*."

Annabel whimpered. "Yes. Yes. Sorry."

Gabriel took a step back as one cold hand left his face and the other released his whimpering companion.

"What are you?" His voice sounded small and insignificant. He had never felt so powerless in all his life.

The figure touched its bald head and a red curl sprang from its scalp. Then another. And another. Gabriel marvelled as luscious hair, the colour of blood, tumbled from its head. Its nose became less narrow and the slit for a mouth grew voluptuous lips. The dark pits of its eyes lightened into a glassy blue. They were the same enchanting colour as Gabriel's.

"I could sense your fear." The figure was now a woman; a slim and beautiful woman with hair that trailed her waistline. "I sense everyone I've bitten. Particularly *you*."

"So it was you!" he cried. "How did you even know I was here? Were you following me? All these years I've hoped to meet you and now, you just show up out of nowhere."

"I always know where you are." She walked around him, the tendrils of her cloak curling and twirling around her as if it were a living thing, feeling its way across the room. "You were my first, Gabriel."

"First?" He kept his eyes pinned on her.

"In the library that day."

He knew it. "Why me?"

She laughed. "So innocent. So naive to the potentials this planet holds. I came here from another world. When I arrived, I was different – altered. I was hungry and you were so full of life. Drinking from you was the first time I discovered how I was to survive here."

Gabriel scowled at her. "Another world? What are you talking about?"

"From beyond the mirror."

"Mirror-?"

"Those who enter the mirror alive will be dead on the other side, such as I. And those who enter the mirror who are *already* dead, will find life waiting for them."

"She's mad!" Annabel quipped and then soared up onto the high window ledge, out of the woman's reach. She didn't much fancy being gripped by the frozen hands of death incarnate again.

Gabriel grabbed the woman's wrist, exerting his strength to distract her from the ghost that cowered above them. "What's beyond the mirror in your world?"

"For you, a human life."

"And Annabel too?"

She nodded; a smile spreading her lips. "Yes. Her too."

"And where is it exactly?"

"Close."

"Tell me."

"Nothing in life – or death – comes free."

"Well, what do you want from me? I have nothing

to give you."

"You do. You have your youth."

He flinched. "You want to take my youth?"

"No, no. I want to *use* it to my advantage."

"Let's go Gabriel. We don't need her," Annabel called down to him.

The vampire ignored the ghost's cries. "Use it how?"

"I want you to go beyond the mirror and find a man for me."

He took a moment to digest this.

"Any man?"

"A *handsome* man. A prince would be perfect, or any kind of nobleman would suffice."

"What's wrong with the men in our world?"

She reached out and moved the black spikes of his fringe with delicate fingers. "I am cursed, boy. All who look upon me in this realm fear and despise me. I cannot love here. I cannot *breathe* here. I am no longer human." Her face rippled into the wrinkled and scarred image of an old man. His eyes were haunting.

"Can't you just go back yourself?"

"I have gone back. Many times. But each time I go, I lose a piece of myself. I am the way I am because my body can no longer hold onto one form."

"And a man will change all that?"

The old man changed once more into the red headed woman but this time, her eyes were full of unshed tears. "I am ready to stop moving around. I want to settle. I want love. You have no idea how hard it is to be unloved for so long."

"I think I do –"

"No. You truly don't." She looked up at Annabel and it became clear to him that though he had never had a girlfriend, or even a first kiss, he had at least had companionship – if you could call it that.

"Do this for me and I'll return these –" From the pocket of her magical cloak, she pulled out his father's pocket watch and Annabel's pendant. It infuriated him to know she'd taken possession of them, but didn't think it wise to argue.

"What if we chose to stay in this new realm you speak of?"

Her eyes flashed crimson. "Then I will venture one last time into the mirror realm and kill you both in the most excruciating way you can imagine."

Annabel joined Gabriel's side, frightened of the crazed woman's words. Gabriel wished he could hold her; to comfort and reassure. He'd always wanted to meet his maker, but not in these circumstances. Would she really hunt him down? Could she really end this eternal life he was forced to endure? He wasn't so sure he wanted to die. Not yet.

"Fine. Tell me where the mirror is…"

Chapter 4

When the location of the mirror was shared with both Gabriel and Annabel, the creature – a human mutation it seemed – disappeared in a cloud of thick, black smoke. When the smoke cleared, Gabriel marvelled at the opening in the bars. There remained a large enough gap for him to escape through, with no evidence of any silver coated iron in his way.

"Are you really doing this?"

He stared at the wall, still in awe of meeting his maker.

"*Gabriel*?"

He blinked. "I guess...We have no choice."

"Yes we do! We can find ourselves a nice pointy stake and ram it in her heart next time she comes sniffing around. We don't need my necklace. I'll stay with you, Gabriel. I've decided I don't want to find out if there's a heaven. I want to be with you forever. Now, can we just get the heck out of here?"

"As sweet as that sounds, Annabel – you need to move on." He left the cell, looking left and right. A long corridor stretched before him both ways. The ghost girl floated close behind him, as always. "Or, if this mirror does what she *says* it does, you could live the life you never had. Wouldn't you like that?"

"What? Grow old and alone in some weird world? No Mum and Dad to make me dinner and tuck me in at night? Forget that! And I know you, Gabriel. You'll leave me as soon as your heart starts beating again."

He took the right corridor.

"Left, you idiot," she prompted.

He swivelled on the balls of his feet, following after her. "I wouldn't leave you. You have my word."

"Fat lot of good your word is. We'll go through that mirror and you'll probably eat me all over again."

Gabriel sighed. He decided it was best not to rise to her complaints any longer. She would only take it as a challenge if he disagreed with her. The sun would be up soon and he wanted to be gone before the town's folk awakened to his escape.

But as he rounded a corner, there came a cry.

"Vampire!"

Gabriel froze as the red-headed boy with the cross bow – one of the party that had helped capture him at the library – approached him; weapon at the ready.

"Not him again," Annabel whined. "Bite him, Gabriel. Because if *you* don't, I'll find a way to, I swear."

Gabriel raised a hand to the boy and spoke calmly. "I'm not going to fight you. I just want to leave this town. I was only passing through but then you put me in that vile cell."

In a slither of moonlight from the high windows, the boy's face appeared to be sweating profusely. He didn't let anything affect his sure and steady stride however.

Gabriel lowered his hand. He would not harm the boy when he came near, but he would certainly maim him if it meant freedom.

"He'll shoot you in the heart. Be careful!" Annabel warned. She had her hands raised over her eyes in an attempt to mask her view, but the translucency of her body made it pointless.

"How did you get out anyway?" the boy demanded. "Those bars are coated with real silver. Cost this town an arm and a leg."

"A friend came," Gabriel replied, "and she'll return for me if she knows you've prevented my escape tonight."

The boy's aim wavered. His voice too. "I can kill you, you know. Pa was going to do it tomorrow night during the festival of the living, but I can just as easily end you now."

Gabriel rolled his eyes. "You humans wear me out."

The boy lowered the crossbow until it was limp in his hands. "We wear each other out."

Annabel hovered behind the boy, staring into his ears. She blew on one and he jerked to the left. She blew on the other, he jerked to the right, spooked by her presence.

"Let me pass."

"Only if you take me with you -"

A prickle of confusion consumed the atmosphere around the vampire. He frowned. "I don't think-"

"Take me with you or I'll ring the bell and scream until everyone comes running."

"Why would you want to come with me? I live a miserable life. It isn't worth it boy, whatever you're running from-"

"I ain't doing Pa's dirty work no more! I hate running around night after night chasing shadows. I wanted to be a dancer. I wanted to sing. He won't let me so much as tap my foot in rhythm without yellin' at me. You're my ticket out of this town. Pretend to hold me hostage, I don't care. Just take me with you."

Annabel crossed her arms over her chest. "I'm not having him following us, Gabriel. I simply won't stand for it. One mangy boy is enough for me to handle."

Gabriel scratched the back of his head. "I don't have time to babysit, kid."

"Babysit! I should clout you for that one!" the boy raged. "I'm a man. I'm my own man and I'll do as I wish. And anyway, you look about the same age as me."

"Be that as it may, my mind is much more mature than yours. I've been around longer than I look."

"Yeah, well I'm coming with you and there's nout more to be said on the matter. Now come with me before Pa wakes up and drags me back to bed by the hair."

Gabriel growled low in his throat. "All right. But just until we reach the border. You're on your own then."

"I say when I'm on my own."

"What's your name anyway? I can't be calling you 'boy' all the time."

"Ginger-nut or nit-wit should do the trick," Annabel said, growing impatient.

"It's Elijah. But call me Eli." Boldly, the boy reached out a hand, to which Gabriel took hold of it in a tight grip.

He did not offer Elijah his own name in return.

"Show me the way out then, Eli. And be quick about it."

*

The town was full of roaming animals. Chickens, geese, goats and pigs all wandered around gobbling up bits of this and that from the floor. Gabriel began to wonder how they kept the livestock safe from Nightcrawlers. It was like an all-you-can-eat buffet.

"Something's been at the pens again and let all the animals out," Eli explained. "While we were taking you to the cell, there must have been another one of those messed up vampire things lurking."

Gabriel grunted in response.

"Here. I took this out of Pa's coat when he was stone drunk." He offered the vial of pig's blood. "Thought you might want it back."

Annabel scowled at the red-head. "Ooh. Look at him being all friendly. You won't need me anymore, now that you've got that stinking blood bag following you around." She spat at the human and the ethereal globule glided through his head. The boy shuddered and glanced over his shoulder momentarily. It was just as well Eli couldn't see or hear the hostile spirit.

Feeling like the human boy's shadow, Gabriel matched his speed as they weaved their way through the town in the direction of the outskirts.

"I need to get to the lake nearby. Do you know of

it?" Gabriel asked when the prison cell was at last well and truly behind him.

Eli nodded. "Yes. But why do you need to go to some stinkin' lake?"

"That business is my own," he replied.

Eli knew all the most secret alley ways and the darkest of corners to hide in as they waited for the occasional human – wandering around in the early hours of the morning, for reasons unknown – that came into visual range. Both vampire and human were slick and quiet; swift and stealthy. Not even the closed eyes of a sleeping cat had peeled open, as they swept by a windowsill where it lay.

"I see sheep. I can't stand sheep," Annabel mumbled, as the two boys vaulted a fence. A sheep and its two lambs were munching on the grass on the border, oblivious to the dangers beyond it.

The sun had gradually risen over the hills, giving the earth some colour and the dew on the grass a sparkle. On the outskirts, a forest of trees swallowed the vampire and his companion, just as the town became completely illuminated with morning rays and the sound of eager cockerels.

"Good timing," Eli said, looking over his shoulder.

Gabriel concurred. "But tell me lad, if you could get around the town so easily, why did you feel you needed to join *me*?"

Eli flinched, but not at Gabriel's question. Just behind the vampire, a Nightcrawler reared its ugly head, teeth long and yellow and eyes red from sleepless nights.

"Because of them!" he yelled, lifting his crossbow and letting an arrow fly. It pierced the Nightcrawler's shoulder, sending it stumbling backwards into the mossy undergrowth. It hissed and screeched as its slender, lengthy fingers clawed at the ground, scrabbling back onto its large bird-like feet.

Gabriel was faster than Eli's second arrow. He moved behind the creatures back and with a precise twist, snapped its brittle neck. It then fell heavily at their feet, just as the arrow hit a tree a short distance away.

"You're faster than me," Eli pointed out. "I'd never survive out here alone."

"Then you should head back. I won't tolerate your company for much longer I'm afraid. I have something I must do-"

"Yeah, you tell him!" Annabel chipped in. She was sitting in a tree, lazily swinging her legs backwards and forwards.

"How do I know you're not plannin' on bringing an army to our town? You could be a scout; a scout for fresh blood." Eli raised his crossbow.

"How do I know you're not leading me into a trap?" Gabriel retorted.

The boys glared at each other, eyes narrowed to slits.

"I guess you'll have to trust me," Eli said.

"I wish I could offer the same sentiment. But I just can't. That's why you should go back, for your own safety."

Eli scowled. "Are you threatening me?"

"I'm warning you."

"Would you pair shut up? This could go on all day. Let's just get to the bleedin' lake, find that old cow her prince, or whatever it was she said she wanted for dinner, and let's get back to normality."

Gabriel sniffed the air. He could smell dirty water, five hundred yards or so away.

"Where are you going?" Eli demanded.

"To the lake."

Eli walked behind the vampire, his strides brisk in order to keep up.

Gabriel shook his head as he walked. There was no winning, was there? He'd gone from looking after one menace, to babysitting another. The good Lord was certainly punishing him for his many crimes.

Chapter 5

Gabriel stared at the vast expanse of liquid, pondering his next move. He then drank from his vial of pig's blood, feeling his veins warm in a moment of renewed life. His heart palpitated for no more than three beats. Then, an ice cold sensation settled once more. For now, he felt less fatigued.

Eli was sat on a muddy hump, chewing on a piece of grass. Annabel was sat next to him, an inch from his side. She was mimicking the human boy, also sporting a piece of grass between her lips. It took Eli a moment to notice the grass floating abnormally beside him and when he did, his eyes widened; his own piece of grass floating to the ground as his lips parted in bemusement. Annabel giggled and continued to torment the boy, enjoying every minute of it. She plucked the grass from her mouth and waved it in front of his eyes, this way and that, making '*wooooo*' noises to accompany the swishing motion of her slender wrist.

"This place is haunted!" Eli cried, trying to swat the blade of grass from the air, to no effect.

"No. It's not. *I* am," Gabriel said.

The water in the lake was murky. It would be hard, once immersed, to locate the mirror. But the vampire's eyes were good and strong; much better than a human's.

"Annabel, are you with me on this?"

Eli looked at Gabriel as if he'd gone barmy.

"Well I'm not staying with this turnip," she said. "And anyway, it hurts me to be away from you too long. You know that."

According to the ghost child, too much distance from the vampire made her ghostly body hum and vibrate with gut wrenching pain. They were connected now. She couldn't leave him, even if she wanted to.

"It's a big lake. It could be anywhere," Gabriel said.

"What are you talkin' about? What could be anywhere? You better start talkin'!" Eli snapped in frustration.

"You wait here with *him*. I'll do the looking," Annabel offered, and dived beneath the cold surface, creating ripples of silvers and browns.

"Why are you just standin' there? What's this all about?" Eli demanded.

"It's about survival. And obligation," Gabriel replied.

"Who were you talking to?"

"A friend."

"What friend? Have you lost your mind?"

"She's someone I killed, a long time ago."

The boy paled. "And she's here?"

"Right now, she's in the lake."

"Why?"

"To find me something important."

"That lake is filled with nothing but reeds and snakes!"

Gabriel closed his eyes. The sunlight warmed his cold, marble-like face, giving him a vague sensation of life. He was calmer now, away from the town, despite the weight of the task that had been laid upon him.

"Found it!" Annabel exclaimed. "It's lying flat on the mud, towards the middle. Come on, let's get this over with."

He nodded and opened his eyes, edging towards the lake. Eli was right. The reeds on the embankment were teaming with snakes, big and small. He kicked one aside and gave the sun one last look before wading out.

The water swirled around him, inching up his stomach, over his chest and finally, over his head. The last thing he heard, before total immersion, was the sound of Eli shouting, "What about me?!"

The fish were great monsters. He'd never seen such brutes before. They lazily sailed by, eyeing Gabriel with big yellow irises, their mouths hanging open in unfriendly smiles. One fish, bigger than his own torso, tried biting his arm clean off. He had to fumble for a rock from the lake bed to smash the creature in the face, sending it shooting away in fear. The other fish glared hungrily at him as he passed silently by.

He trudged onwards. His shoes sank in the mud. It was a real effort to move and he soon found himself swimming instead; his mouth full of the bitter tasting water that was also swishing around in his empty, useless lungs.

Annabel's body was glowing, providing a

miniscule amount of light. She was gesturing frantically, leading Gabriel through a maze of waving reeds. When at last the ghost stood still, pointing to something ahead, he sighed inwardly.

It was big. The frame was as thick as Gabriel's forearm, brown with flecks of a once gold plated frame. The mirror was filthy and cracked, but in the dim light of Annabel's glow, he could see his own face staring back at him. It was the only mirror he'd ever discovered that could bear a vampire's reflection. A ghost-child's too.

He gave her a thumbs up.

She smiled.

He placed a hand against the glass, expecting to touch its solid surface, but the soft flesh of his fingers disappeared inside his own reflection.

Annabel gasped. "The old bag was telling the truth."

He nodded and manoeuvred himself directly above the mirror.

It began to brighten.

"Gabriel, are you sure?" she asked.

No. He wasn't sure. He wasn't sure of anything anymore. Just when he thought he had a tight grasp on his reality, a figure in a cloak with a changing face showed up, talking of magic mirrors; altering his perceptions. And here the mirror lay, on the bed of an abandoned lake, just like she'd promised.

He propelled himself forwards with both arms and legs, feeling his face pass through the mirror's surface. It suddenly felt as if needles were pricking at his skin – digging into his eye sockets and his ear drums. His vision filled with colours, every shade, blending and blurring together. And still he moved on, until the swimming became a stomach lurching fall.

*

Gabriel lay on his back; a crescent moon hanging starkly in a pitch sky. His ears were ringing and his head pounded, but a smile crossed his lips none the less - for he could feel his heart beating wildly in his chest.

"Gabriel?" came the nervous whisper of a girl beside him. One of her pigtails had loosened – blonde hair tumbling over her narrow shoulders on one side in an awkward fashion – and her milky white face was covered in mud. "Did it work?"

He reached out a warm hand to her face and felt the soft flesh of a living being. Annabel was solid – *alive* – and for the first time since he'd killed her many years ago, he could smell the life on her skin.

"We're breathing." He felt for his pulse, pushing fingers into his neck, then reached out and felt for Annabel's. "We're actually alive!"

She jumped to her feet and began bouncing up and down. "It worked! It worked!" She danced around Gabriel, her feet leaving indentations in the soft mud around them.

It was then that Gabriel noticed the mirror in which they'd passed through. It was propped against a tree on a hillock, reflecting the moon. But why would such a sacred object go unguarded? They were in the open, on a marsh it seemed. The ground surrounding the hillock was boggy and the skyline, vacant of any huts or houses.

"We're in the middle of nowhere," he muttered.

"And my belly is as hungry as a starving dogs. What shall I eat first? We can eat cream cakes and warm bread, honey glazed parsnips and sweets! Oh, my aching belly. Come on Gabriel, let's find someplace to eat. Just think, no more blood dinners for you-"

Gabriel smiled, but only half-heartedly. As much as he revelled in the sensation of oxygen filling his lungs and carbon dioxide escaping them, he did not appreciate the feeling of an impending death. The creature with the changing faces would return for him if he did not bring back a lover.

This life could be very short-lived.

"It's so dark. We should maybe stay a while until the sun rises."

"No way! I'm going!" Annabel lifted the hem of her dress and began wading through the murky waters. She had taken three steps before a sudden scream tore from her mouth.

"What? What is it?" Gabriel rushed to her side and pulled her away. When she was safely behind him, he peered down into the water. What at first seemed like a dead fish, with many unnatural fins, caught the moonlight and revealed itself to be a human hand, severed at the wrist.

"A hand! Someone's hand! What's it doing there?"

Gabriel stared at it. Maybe a great battle had been fought here? And as he pictured an army tearing its enemies to shreds before his very eyes, he noticed that all around them, hands twisted and bobbed in the filthy bog. They rested on the dirty liquid surface with bulbous swellings of the knuckles.

"They're everywhere." A mild terror flitted through him.

Annabel let out a little whine. "I can't look." She raised her hands to shield her face and Gabriel squeezed her arm in comfort.

"We'll stay here, by the mirror, till daylight. When we can see better, to make a safe path through the bog, we'll head north."

"Maybe we should just...go back through the mirror?" she asked hesitantly.

"We just got here."

"Yes, but it's scary here! I think I'd rather be a ghost again."

He frowned. "And what would you have me say to my maker?"

"That we couldn't find anyone because all their hands have been chopped off!"

Gabriel settled beneath the tree, avoiding physical contact with the mirror. The last thing he wanted was to fall through and have to swim around in that ghastly lake on the other side again.

"We wait until morning, then we head north."

Annabel pouted and slumped next to him, her soggy, wet dress bunching up around her skinny legs. The long white socks that met her knees were now black with dirt.

"This will be the death of us," she grumbled.

"Second times the charm," he replied, and closed his eyes on the moon.

Chapter 6

The sun that rose that morning burned a sickly green colour, giving the world a strange and sombre hue. Birds the size of large dogs flew overhead, terrorizing Annabel from her sleep. They were turquoise in colour and instead of squawking with the arrival of a new morning, they let rip a wheezy barking that could be heard for miles around.

"Have they gone?" Annabel squeaked, her hands over her eyes.

Gabriel pressed her head to his chest, his mouth agape as he marvelled at the creatures. They dipped low, swooping so close he could see their underbellies and four clawed feet.

"They've passed," he assured her, stroking her hair. The blonde strands were soft and golden, with a few copper strands in the mix. It felt strange, being able to hold her again. She was so young and fragile; just how he remembered her that night in the park. His hands trembled.

"I've never seen such big birds before."

Her stomach rumbled and she clutched it in embarrassment. Gabriel took her hand and squeezed it. "I'll look for something we can eat just as soon as we find dry land."

"I'm not putting my legs back in that bog," she told him, crossing her arms in defiance. She hadn't got much sleep in the night and was feeling cranky; more cranky than usual.

"You can go back through the mirror and wait on the other side if you want? It's your choice."

She looked behind Gabriel at the huge mirror propped against the dry bark of the tree. The mirror's tarnished frame seemed insignificant in the green haze of light falling upon it. It seemed hard to believe it was the most miraculous discovery they'd ever made. But there it was, in all its splendour.

"If I go back through, I'll change again, right? I don't much like being alone."

"Well, Eli's probably still waiting by the river, wondering where the heck we got to. Torment him for a bit if you're bored."

She raised her chin, poking her nose into the air. "No. I'll stay. But you'll have to carry me."

Gabriel had anticipated this. It was the least he could do for her. "Fine. Hop on." He bent his knees and gestured for her to climb aboard, which she did in an impressive leap. Her thin arms laced around his chest and her skinny legs gripped onto his waist. She was light – not quite as weightless as when she was dead – but light enough not to cause him too much discomfort.

"Hold tight."

"Well I wasn't going to hold on any other way," she snorted.

He began wading through the sea of severed

hands, which floated forlornly in the murk; swollen mitts that looked deathly pale.

"They're disgusting." Annabel's breath tickled his ear as she spoke.

"It's not a pretty sight, for sure."

"Who did this?"

"A very angry individual, or a creature of some sort, I guess."

"Maybe they're a sacrifice?"

"I'd hate to think what god these people believe in, if they require hands as sacrifice to-"

The conversation cut short as Gabriel's foot disappeared into deeper water. It slipped in the muddy bed and as he tried righting himself, Annabel let rip a squeal of surprise. Water swallowed Gabriel's entire body and Annabel, crying out, was immersed from the neck down. The severed hands surrounded them instantly, jostled from the waves created by their flailing limbs. They brushed against Annabel's cheek and the fingers of one entangled in her sopping hair.

"Ah! Get it off me! Get it off me!" she wailed.

Gabriel resurfaced in a wild leap, sending water and hands flying in all directions.

"I'm sorry," he said, spitting out dirty fluid. "I slipped."

"You idiot!" she bellowed in his ear. "I want to go back. Take me back, Gabriel."

There was no chance he would return to the mirror now.

"We can't."

"*Please.*"

"No."

He moved onwards in what he assumed was a straight line, managing to stay upright for the duration.

When a third of the day had passed, wading through sludge, at last a smattering of tall, leafy trees reared their heads on the horizon.

"Land," Annabel cheered. "And trees. Ooh, I can't wait to get out of this smelly bog."

Gabriel was about to point out that, besides the mishap hours previous, she was nowhere near the water. It was *he* who had hands and filth up to his middle. But with dry earth in his field of vision, he felt only the need to push his legs through that last stretch.

"Oh, sweet safety!" Annabel cried, kissing the earth.

It was flat and dry, blossoming with wild flowers of pinks and yellows. The trees bore leaves of red and gold, reminding Gabriel of Annabel's hair as she bobbed about the place, merrily. But her enthusiasm was short-lived when a tree began to move. Its thick branches lumbered downwards, one of which plonked the girl on the head in warning as she poked a hole through a hanging hive.

A swarm of bees spewed from the hive's puncture wound and they dived at their intruder. Annabel yelled and yelled as the trees around her came alive, slender braches swatting at the small, persistent insects. The buzzing sound increased as the bee's fury was made known and then it softened. The insects were knocked clean out of the air, crushed beneath tree bark.

Gabriel was on the floor, curled around a quaking

Annabel protectively. If he moved, he feared the trees would swat him too. But when the forest became still, he cautioned a glance upwards. It appeared all was quiet.

"Is it safe?" she whispered.

He rose slowly.

The trees seemed uninterested now that the frenzy was over.

He rubbed his forehead, where a nasty lump had arisen. The sting there had been painful and the aftermath, itchy. But the grass was littered with the dying bees. None, it seemed, had survived.

"Let's keep moving," he urged, picking Annabel up and setting her onto her feet once more.

They hurried onwards, stomachs growling. Annabel kept as close to Gabriel as she could, watching the trees closely for signs of life. She also made sure to watch the floor at intervals, in case she tripped on a suspiciously raised root.

When the pair stumbled upon a single house made of logs and thatch, relief brimmed in their stomachs. Caught up in the moment of such a familiar 'human' thing, Annabel stormed ahead, long before Gabriel had the chance to tell her it was unwise. She skipped right up to the door, unabashed by the houses' bizarre windowless structure.

"Anyone home?" she sang through the gap, for the door was ajar and 'clacking' as it bounced against its wooden frame.

Gabriel gripped her shoulder and tugged her backwards from the small wooden porch, just as an old man shuffled out. Annabel let out a little gasp as she took a step closer.

"One hand," she breathed. "He's got one hand." She gripped a hold of Gabriel's fingers in a tight squeeze of panic.

The man's wrist was red with scar tissue, poking from the sleeve of an off-white crinkled shirt. Sweat patches were visible at the armpits. The man looked old; a thick, grey beard consuming the lower half of his face.

"I want no trouble, you hear me?" he said gruffly, waving the one hand that was still intact. "Get away now."

Annabel looked up at him in instant disgust. "Hang on a minute. You haven't given us a chance to introduce ourselves." She turned to Gabriel for support. He was motionless, waiting in anticipation of hostility from the stranger.

"Let's leave him be," he mumbled, beginning to pull the little girl away.

"But we're starving. We haven't eaten in *hundreds* of years, Gabriel." She rounded on the old man, who flinched as her pigtails spun outwards like a propeller. "Can't you give us something to eat? We're desperate. A bit of toast, with jam if you've got any? But if you only have butter, that will do."

The old man glowered at her as if she were a pesky rat, nipping at his heels. "I have barely two crumbs to feed myself, she-devil."

She clutched her belly. It rumbled, as if on cue.

"If you don't have any food, good sir, do you know where we can find some?" Gabriel intervened.

The old man pointed his ugly stump towards a

path through the trees. "Follow that road." He started to leave.

"Hey! What happened to your hand?" Annabel asked, before he could disappear back inside his little, windowless house.

Gabriel rubbed a palm over his face and sighed. Annabel would never learn to hold her tongue. He would have to sit her down and explain that there was a time and place for questions. This wasn't one of them.

The old man's brow furrowed. "Are you so uneducated?" He bent down to meet her gaze.

"I was wondering, is all. We had to swim through a lot of hands to get here."

His eyes darted towards Gabriel. "Travellers?"

"Yes."

"And you know nothing of the King and his daughters?"

Gabriel stared blankly ahead, which was answer enough for the old man.

"Ooh, a King?" Annabel chirped excitably. "How fun, like a fairy tale. I remember those. Sort of-"

He scrutinised the young, babbling girl with contempt. It seemed 'fun' wasn't how he'd phrase it. "I noticed you have your hands." He gestured to Gabriel. "A rare sight in these parts. If I were you lad, I'd be on my merry way before you lose them both. And take the wee one with you."

"We can't go back. Not yet."

"Are you thieves? Are you wanted? If so, you can get away from here. I'll whisper to the trees and have them knock your block off for trespassing."

"Do I look like a thief?" Annabel cut in.

"Skinny little thing like you, who knows?"

She scowled at him stubbornly, forcing as many wrinkles into her brow as were displayed on the head of the one-handed man. Hers were not quite as deep.

"We aren't thieves. We are merely looking for work," Gabriel lied. "And I'm sorry we disturbed you."

"Then let me warn you," the man replied, his voice deep. "Avoid eye contact with people. You just might fix your gaze upon the King's two daughters, Floriana and Rosemary. They walk among us, sometimes surrounded by their royal guard and sometimes, freely. But they're cursed."

Annabel was silent; her attention hooked on his every word. Gabriel was equally as attentive, worry slithering down his spine.

"If you look into their eyes, you'll instantly want them with a fiery passion. Through any means necessary you'll try and lay hands on their ivory skin. And if you do, well..." He raised his stump. "The King will take your hand. Both of them if you're stupid enough to fall under their spell twice."

Annabel gasped.

"I moved here to be away from the she-devils. I have my one good hand. A painter needs his hand."

"Why don't you leave this place?"

"Nothing to live on. Not much chance of getting a job now. I'm old. I've become set in my ways and I like the isolation."

"Well, why don't you come back with us?" Annabel asked, in a flash of (what she thought was) brilliance.

"Annabel," Gabriel hissed.

"What was that, girl?" the man spurred.

"Would you like a wife?"

"Stop it," the ex-vampire growled.

"What? We came here for a man and we've found one," she whispered.

The old man cocked his head to the side, straining to hear her. "What are you talking about? I won't marry a child."

"No. Not *me*."

Gabriel reached out and placed a hand over her mouth. Her words distorted as she desperately tried explaining herself.

"I want no woman," the old man barked at them. "They're all she-devils."

"We're sorry for disturbing you," Gabriel apologised, edging away.

Annabel tugged his hand from her mouth and yelled, "If you just came back and looked at her, maybe you'd change your mind."

"Quiet," Gabriel scolded.

The old man walked to his front door and slammed it behind him.

"Tell me, Annabel. Do you really think that *thing* back in our world would want a one-handed painter, content with living in a sizeable *shed*?"

"I thought I was doing you a favour. We could have gone straight home and been on our way if he'd said yes."

He shook his head. It pounded with pain and his

aching stomach accompanied it. With little more to gain from lingering there, he put his hand on her shoulder and steered her away, granting the old man some peace. They took the path – the only clear trodden passage through the forest – and wondered if they'd ever find the perfect suitor for Gabriel's blood thirsty maker.

Chapter 7

"Will you promise me something?" Gabriel asked.

"Maybe."

He gripped Annabel's shoulders and gave her a practised glare. When he was a vampire, he could stare at people with such intensity, it held his victims in a state of paralysis. But as a human, his stare only made the little girl feel inferior.

"Don't say anything out of turn when we reach this Kingdom. I'll do all the talking."

"But what if someone speaks to me first?"

"Then I'll tell them you're a mute, so they'll no longer feel the need to encourage you." He let go of her and cautiously brushed aside the lower branches of the trees that were obstructing their way. Annabel, a significant amount shorter than him, was capable of ducking under most of them. *These* trees seemed quiet at least –- unmoving – though he trusted them no more. "Oh, and if anyone asks," he added. "Tell them I'm your brother."

"Why?"

"Because they'll find it strange otherwise."

"Why's that?"

"Because a teenage boy walking around with an

unrelated minor is suspicious. They'll wonder why you're with me."

"Tell them I'm your slave. I bet you'd love that, wouldn't you? Someone to brush your hair every morning."

He rolled his eyes.

"And anyway," she said, "how can I tell them you're my brother if I'm not allowed to speak?"

He smirked. "I was testing you."

"Humph!" She bent down and picked up a fallen branch, using it as a walking stick. *I'm a great explorer*, she thought, *travelling through foreign lands on a troublesome quest*. Her stick made her feel older and more sophisticated, like an aged monk scaling a mountain top in search of answers. She was doing just that. Seeking answers. And Gabriel was her stupid sidekick. *Yes, that's right,* she decided. *A big stupid sidekick, who has cut out my tongue so I can't talk to strangers.*

"Stop that," Gabriel said.

Annabel swung her stick like a sword, whacking daisy heads from their stems. She pummelled a tree stump, glowering up into the branches and wondering if the tree could feel her blows. She wanted it to move again. She wanted to feel the rush of danger, like all explorers did.

"Annabel!" Gabriel grabbed the broken tree branch in mid swing. "I won't be able to hear what's coming –"

She let go of the branch and sulkily kicked a purple flower that was trembling in the breeze. Gabriel, the spoiler of all fun. Where was his sense of adventure? She'd always been the careful one as a ghost. Funny how now – when she could get severely harmed at the turn of every corner – she felt like the strong and indestructible heroine of her own wild story.

"This isn't the time or place for games. What that man said back there… it's frightening."

She saw the fear in his eyes and stilled.

"I'm sorry," she croaked in a small voice.

"That's okay."

They embraced. Gabriel patted her gently on the back, and on parting he pushed her hurriedly behind him.

A queer shape had moved into his line of vision, beyond the lower branches of a cluster of pines, just a short distance ahead. Annabel spotted the figure also and gripped Gabriel's bicep, feeling safe in the knowledge he was bigger and stronger than most boys his age.

His first thought was *Princess*. But would a princess be permitted to scope the woods alone? It seemed unlikely. Gabriel made the decision to slip deeper into the shadows of the forest before they could be detected, but the figure moved suddenly in a swish of garments. It was a woman he could see; a young woman, with a wicker basket under her arm (hence the queer shape she'd made in the distance). And like a startled deer, she turned to them with the snapping of twigs beneath feet.

Gabriel remained frozen. His mind was in turmoil. Should he advance? Or should he wait for her to approach? He didn't know. He considered asking her out-right if she was of royal blood.

While he thought about what he should do, the girl dropped her basket and rumpled up the many layers of a raggedy gown, which hung loosely from her boney shoulders. At her ankle, tied to her skin with a leather strap, was a small sheathed dagger. As she raised it in her fist, the blade glinted in the fading green light of day.

"Wait," Gabriel called. "We're not here to harm you."

The woman bent her frame so that her long brown hair tumbled downwards, nearly stroking the ground on which she tread so carefully. Her feet were bare, Gabriel noticed, as she inched through the mêlée of swooping branches towards them.

"If I tell you to run, do so," he whispered to Annabel sharply.

"She's just a girl," she pointed out, though it was more to convince herself than any other.

"Who are you?" growled the stranger. She moved her dagger mere inches from Gabriel's neck.

He swallowed, his pulse thumping loudly.

She was a beautiful creature, if not terrifying. Her slate grey eyes were full of a wild and unpredictable intent as she scrutinised both he and Annabel.

"We're travellers. That's all. We just want to get to the Kingdom before dark."

"No one comes this way. If you had, you would have waded through the sea of hands. No one bothers to get their pretty feet wet in such a grotesque swamp."

"We did," Annabel insisted. "Well, actually, he carried me."

The woman seemed to mull this information over

in her head. The dagger lowered a fraction in her hand, until she realised her practised poise had slipped, jutting it upwards once more.

"Only dishonourable men sneak up on a woman," she barked, taking a step closer to them.

Gabriel could feel the tip of the blade against his flesh. He could smell the earthy scent that clung to the girl's skin and see the dirt in the ridges of her skeletal frame. She was beautiful in face – perfectly arched eyebrows, a petite and slightly upturned nose and full red lips – but she also looked starved; gaunt even.

"We were just as surprised as you were," Gabriel replied.

"How do I know you're not spies?"

"Spies!" Annabel exclaimed.

Gabriel felt the child move out from behind him. Her hot temper was brewing again and he could do nothing to still her tongue when a blade was so close to penetrating his main artery. Even in his current predicament, he couldn't fail to see the irony in this.

The woman slid a cold hand around his throat. Gabriel's chest swelled in preparation for any pain she meant to cause, but her eyes were fixed upon the little girl now, watching her with interest.

"We came all this way through that smelly, boggy water and I'm not going to let you ruin everything now. So unhand him."

The woman chuckled, which alarmed the ex-vampire, who was at her mercy. "Brave little soul aren't you?" she said, then turned to Gabriel. With a quick flick of her wrist, she pressed the edge of the dagger into his skin, drawing blood. He sucked in a sharp intake of breath. There came a cry of "No!" from Annabel. The woman then pushed Gabriel hard in the chest and retreated backwards a few steps, licking the blade with her tongue.

Was she a vampire? No, surely not?

Gabriel lay amongst the grass, waiting for her fangs to appear; waiting for her to finish him off. But she just smiled, bent down gracefully and placed the dagger safely back in its sheath.

"Human," she concluded.

"Excuse me?" he said.

"Your blood. It's human."

Annabel rushed to Gabriel's aid, placing her little hands on his neck and right collarbone. She checked that there were no gaping wounds; afraid that the woman might have stabbed him someplace, as well as pricked his flesh. When her analysis of his torso was complete, she was satisfied that Gabriel had been unharmed.

"I trust that you are human too?" the woman asked.

Annabel flinched, worried that the woman might bring her dagger out again and slice her too.

"Of course I am!" she yelled. "Why didn't you just ask us, instead of waving that knife around?"

"Why do you care?" Gabriel asked. "What does it even matter to you?"

The woman was moving backwards on the balls of her feet. The trees had come alive again, moving their branches for her – granting her a clear path to her wicker basket that lay neglected in a flower bed. "I knew you were travellers, because you, boy, had both hands. But forgive me, I find it strange you would wish to come here. This place is a dark land. I thought you might have been supernatural beings of some sort. You can never be too careful."

Gabriel scrambled to his feet. Annabel found his hand and squeezed it tightly.

"We're hungry, that's all," Gabriel explained.

"I'm sure you are," the woman called over her shoulder as she retrieved the basket. "If your business here is merely to fill your bellies, continue along this path. You might just catch the market. The gypsies and farmers provide most of the produce for our great Kingdom." She said 'great' in a sarcastic drawl.

Keen to leave, Gabriel and Annabel hurried onwards, having no choice but to pass the woman as they went. She smiled at them, a cold and mirthless smile that chilled their blood.

"A word of advice!" she shouted after them, before they were completely out of sight, "Tie a rag around your eyes boy and let the girl lead you. I'm sure you value your hands!"

Laughter followed them.

Chapter 8

There were so few men about. This was Gabriel's first thought when he came upon a thriving market, with Annabel in tow. The few men who were amongst gossiping females kept their heads down and eyes to the floor; wrist stumps swinging uselessly at their hips. It was a sorry sight to see.

"So many sad people here," Annabel whispered, clutching onto Gabriel's arm even tighter.

The wooden buildings were two storeys high with big porches – much like those in Gabriel's world. There were no vehicles however, only wagons and hoof marks from horses and donkeys. The floor was sludgy in places, though generally safe to walk on without sinking too deep into dirt. It hadn't rained since their passage through the mirror, and Gabriel didn't speculate as to why moisture pooled here and there on the ground.

In some areas, people had set up tents and marquees. Goods were laid out on blankets at their feet or rickety tables covered in cloth. There was so much to see and smell – so many people calling and luring customers in. Even as the green tinted sky darkened to ebony, there was little discouragement in people, from making a sale. Flaming torches were eventually positioned on posts, lighting the way.

"Ooh, look at these!" Annabel dragged Gabriel to a table. It bore steaming pies with a crisp brown pastry that begged to be eaten.

"We have no money, Annabel," he reminded her solemnly.

"You like?" asked a woman, with a curiously skeletal upper body and a slightly puffy middle. Her teeth were mottled with black stains that obliterated Gabriel's appetite somewhat. "Rat pies. A penny for two?"

"Yeesh!" Annabel drew her hand away hurriedly. "Do you have anything that *isn't* rat?"

The woman gestured to the pies at the back of the table. "Crocodile?"

"Oh. Um, that's all right." She raised her empty hands in decline and scurried along.

"Wait up!" Gabriel called. "You're getting ahead of yourself here. We should be looking for a place we can sleep tonight." Sleep. It dawned on him now how unusual that sounded. He hadn't slept in so many years now, the idea of it seemed foreign. Even the previous night – after his body had altered through the mirror and come alive as if he'd never been bitten – he'd only managed to wink in and out of unconsciousness. He'd been too afraid to take his eyes off the little girl beside him.

"You said we had no money."

"We don't."

"So where can we sleep?"

"Make way for Princess Floriana!" came a bellow.

The cheerful expressions on the women's faces melted and the sombre eyes of the men flickered with terror.

Annabel reacted with great speed, yanking on Gabriel's arm and coaxing him to his knees where she then wrapped her arms around him from behind. With her fingers pressed tightly together, she placed them over his eyes.

"Don't even *think* about looking at her!" she hissed.

The people around them were bending to one knee, in respect of the Princess's entrance into the market. But Annabel didn't move, in fear of granting Gabriel a peak at her highness upon a white horse.

Princess Floriana was nothing like Annabel had imagined she would be. Her brown hair was curled up in a bun about her head and her long, gangly limbs looked frightfully unnatural. Her complexion had a sickly, greasy texture and her thick eyebrows met in the middle.

"She's an ugly one," Annabel mumbled.

Princess Floriana commanded her horse to stop with a yip and pull of the reins. Her guards on similar steeds paused alongside her, their bodies clothed in silver armour, like that of a knight's. When Princess Floriana slid her giant feet from the stirrups, one of her guards left their own horse to help her to the ground. She dropped with a thud. The guard at her side shed their helmet.

It seemed the Princess's guard were not men at all – as one might have assumed. They were women. All of them; strong, muscular women!

"Why do you not kneel before me?!" the Princess

growled. She had a husky voice – quite unladylike.

"I would have…um…your majesty, it's just my *brother* here might look at you and then…well…your dad would chop his hands off. And…I like his hands."

"Insolent child!" Floriana wrenched at Annabel's wrists, prying her fingertips from Gabriel's face. He flinched at the movement, but was wise to keep his eyes tightly shut. "On your knees!"

"Do as she says," Gabriel advised.

Annabel hitched her dress up and sunk down onto the wooden porch, desperately biting back a retort. She thanked the Lord that there were no cursed Princesses back in their own world.

"You're new here," Floriana said. "I can tell." She was dressed in a cream smock with silver leggings that bore spots of crimson here and there. From her horse's saddle, two pheasants hung, dripping their life fluid over the horse's white flank.

Annabel scowled as Floriana gripped Gabriel by the chin, turning his face from side to side to get a good look at his wonderfully high cheek bones and the dark circles under his eyes.

"Yes. You're new. I would have remembered a face like yours." The lids of Gabriel's eyes trembled as she leaned closer. She let rip a great laugh, directly in his face. "I think I might have to come back for you at some point. Won't my sister be disappointed to know I saw you first."

Annabel chewed the skin inside her lip. Oh, the things she wanted to say! But she didn't. She knew Gabriel would be angry and she hated it when he was disappointed in her. He was the closest thing she had to a family. She vaguely remembered having a talented older sibling that her parents favoured more, when she was alive. She'd always been left out. But Gabriel had never left her. Never.

"What is your name?"

He flinched. He hated that question.

"Caleb," he lied, thinking it would be wise to keep his identity close to his heart – for the time being. It was a strange land for sure and he did not want anyone having an inkling of power over him.

"I'll be seeing you again, Caleb. Come. Back to the Kingdom!" Floriana snapped her fingers and the female knight to her left moved as if a key had been wound and suddenly released in her back. She clomped noisily to the horses, lifted the Princess to her saddle and away they went; watched only by the females of the kingdom.

Annabel sighed and climbed to her feet. "She. Was. *Scary*."

"That was a close call."

"My heart was beating so fast! I thought she was going to force your eyes open." Annabel flung herself onto Gabriel, hugging him around his waist. "I'm so glad you didn't look." He stroked her hair and squeezed her tiny body to him.

The people of the Kingdom stirred slowly – their bones shaken by the intrusion. The Princess made them skittish, without a shadow of a doubt. It was infectious. Gabriel could feel her spell lingering and it unsettled him.

An elderly man with filmy white eyes clapped a stump on Gabriel's shoulder.

"You're a lucky boy. Most would have felt the pull of the witches spell upon them and opened their eyes in her presence."

"I could feel it," Gabriel nodded. "It's so strong."

The man nodded in return. "You must be made of stronger stuff than I." He pointed his stump at a table of bread. "Take a loaf. My wife makes them. No payment necessary."

Annabel didn't need telling twice. She swooped upon a loaf and began tearing at the thick crust with her teeth.

"But just so you know," the man added, "She will return for you. You're a handsome lad… the Princess will not forget a face."

"I don't plan on sticking around for long," Gabriel replied.

"Wise."

"I don't suppose you know of a place we can stay for the night? I can be of some use to your home I'm sure, as payment. I'm strong, like you said."

The old man sighed. "I wish I could be so kind, but you're a marked lad. No one will want you. The Princess said she will return for you and no sane gentleman would risk keeping you around if that be the case."

"So, when does the spell wear off? Or curse, to be more accurate? Surely men won't forever desire the Princesses?" He asked this only because the men with severed limbs in the market had all executed restraint in her presence just now.

"No. No. It lasts a matter of days. The King will keep you imprisoned for the duration of it. And you'll go mad with desire the whole time you're locked up. It'll make you claw at the walls, begging for one touch of her hair, her skin. And you know the rest I'm sure."

Gabriel took the half of a loaf of bread being offered to him by Annabel. She was smiling whilst chewing, satisfied that the ache in her stomach was at last ebbing away.

"Did I hear you say you needed shelter, in return for working?"

Gabriel clamped his eyes shut at the sound of a feminine voice disturbing the peace. Could it be the second Princess? He did not want to risk a glimpse of her.

"You're all right boy. She won't hurt you," the old man assured him.

Peeling open one blue eye, Gabriel saw the bare footed woman from the woods, with her basket of herbs. She stood on the dirt road, looking up at him.

"Hello again," he said. "I didn't expect to-"

"I live on the outskirts," she cut in. "I could do with some help if you're willing? It is a rare sight, seeing two hands. I realised back in the woods, once you'd left, that I could accommodate you."

"And the little one too?" He drew Annabel to him. They were a package deal.

"Aye. If you wish it."

He nodded in gratitude.

Annabel's jaw opened a little wider than she'd intended. The woman with the long brown hair had been so hostile when they'd first crossed paths and yet now, she wanted to help them! Why did she have to come along with that pretty heart shaped face of hers and those big emerald eyes? She should just…go away!

"That's ok. We have a place to stay already," Annabel said.

"You do?" She looked surprised. "But I-"

"Annabel!" Gabriel snapped. "What are you playing at?"

Annabel scowled at him, chewing slowly on her mouthful.

"Forgive her. She's tired. A long day, as you can imagine. I would be incredibly grateful if you could help us."

The young woman reached a hand out to the boy. "I'm Seren."

"G-aleb," he replied. His cheeks reddened, having almost revealed his true name. "Caleb Waters. And this is Annabel."

"Are you done here?" Seren asked.

"Yes."

"But I haven't finished looking!" Annabel snapped childishly.

"The market is always here. You can come back another day," Seren said.

And as Gabriel joined the young woman's side, Annabel followed close behind, poking her wet, pink tongue out at them both, every chance she got.

Chapter 9

Seren lived in a mud hut. It was surrounded by tall grass and big daisies that bobbed their heads in the evening breeze. The thickening darkness made the hut seem deceptively small but inside, it was rather spacious and welcoming. There was a wooden table, big enough to seat four; a work top spread with tools and cutlery beneath a window; a bed of thick and colourful blankets, amongst which a brown bear skin lay; a wood burner nestled in a corner and a general assortment of odds and ends such as books on shelves and an empty bucket.

"You live alone?" Gabriel wondered, as Seren pointed at the table for them to sit around.

Her silence gave him the impression he'd spoken out of turn.

"I do now, yes. But that wasn't always the case." She dropped her basket on the work top and pulled a ribbon from a pocket in her dress. With it, she tied her long brown hair back from her face. "I had a husband once."

Annabel looked to Gabriel. He was listening intently, his body rigid in his chair – a trait he had mastered in death and apparently still held onto in rebirth.

"He said, if he couldn't have the Princess, he couldn't stay here any longer."

"I thought the spell wore off eventually?" Gabriel wondered, watching her closely.

"It was before the curse was even laid upon the King's daughters," she explained, with sadness in the lull of her voice.

"But she's so ugly!" Annabel piped up.

"Not Floriana," Seren replied stiffly. "Princess Rosemary."

The silence of still tongues grew heavy for a moment. They could hear the call of a tawny owl outside and the rustle of the wind through the grass.

"She was only twelve. Twelve! She was out with her brother in the market one day. He saw her and told me he was in love."

"How horrid!" Annabel said.

"He used to talk about her to me. His own wife! He used to tell me he would wait for the Princess to come of age before asking for her hand in marriage."

Gabriel felt sympathy bubble in his chest for the young woman. He couldn't imagine how terrible it must be, to love someone who blatantly loves another. And to do so in marriage too. It was wrong.

"But in the end, the waiting got to him. He told me I was nothing compared to Princess Rosemary… that he hated the very sight of me. He left for the Kingdom and broke into her chamber."

Annabel held her breath.

"The King wanted him executed, but my husband got away. He didn't stop here to say goodbye. I had to hear it from a maid on her day off from work at the palace that he'd left me once and for all."

Seren started rifling through the blankets.

"So they have a brother?" Annabel asked suddenly.

Gabriel turned to the little girl, whose legs swung backwards and forwards on the chair, much like she'd done when she were a ghost.

Seren nodded from across the room. "Prince Delwyn."

"Is he handsome?"

"Very handsome, yes." Her tone had brightened some.

"Is he cursed?"

"No child. We can gaze freely at him."

"Maybe we could bring him back home, Gabriel?"

Gabriel flinched.

"You said your name was Caleb?" Seren said, bundling blankets up close to her chest. She didn't sound entirely angry or suspicious as Gabriel's cheeks reddened. "It's okay," she continued. "Many use different names on passing through here."

"I'm sorry," Gabriel said. "I didn't mean to keep secrets from you, it's just-"

"Princess Floriana wants to make you her new toy? I heard her. It's alright. I will call you Caleb if you wish."

"Call me Gabriel. It's pointless lying in your company."

She nodded. "Now, take these. You can sleep by

the wood burner."

Gabriel set up Annabel's bed first. The little girl watched him tentatively as he spread out the blankets, gesturing for her to lay closest to the fire, so she wouldn't feel the draught coming through the cracks in the front door. From the corner of his eye, he noticed Seren was watching him as she chopped the herbs she'd gathered in the woods; an amused expression playing on her lips.

Annabel curled in a ball. She glanced over her shoulder to check Gabriel was nearby and with her face towards the flames, placed her thumb in her mouth. As she did, her mind came awash with memories of her past life – of her bedroom full of china dolls, staring eerily down at her from a shelf her father had put up at a jaunty angle. She'd hated those dolls. She also remembered how she'd sucked hard on her thumb until it was wrinkly, whilst her parents argued downstairs deep into the night.

"Are you all right?" Gabriel whispered, hearing a gasp escape the little girl's mouth.

"Yes," she assured him, then returned her thumb to the moist bed of her tongue.

"You don't have to be afraid," he added. "I'm right here beside you."

She closed her eyes as Gabriel nestled down next to her. He lay on his back, staring up at the ceiling. The sound of the knife on the counter chopped through the air. Shadows danced around the room like restless spirits.

When Seren was done, she scooped the herbs into a jar and returned it to the shelf, wiping her hands on her dress. "I'm not far if you need me. There's drinking water in the bucket if you're thirsty and if you need to relieve yourselves, there's a toilet out back beyond the cabbage patch. But if you stand on my vegetables in the dark, I'll know about it. And I won't be in the best of moods."

Gabriel was unsure whether Seren was joking about the vegetables, but smiled anyway. Slowly, she smiled back and then left for an adjoining room, gazing over at her guests one last time before closing the wooden door behind her.

He could hear her moving around; the subtle swish of material as her dress was shed and the rustling of blankets as she prepared to sleep. Gabriel, himself, was tired now. He could feel it. He'd never felt as incredibly relaxed as he did right then. Or at least, he couldn't remember the last time he'd felt this comfortable. The sensation of heat on his skin was a welcoming companion in the night and his inner turmoil of thoughts and worries lessened with his waning consciousness. He drifted on a cloud of relief, basking in the coming darkness and like an extinguished flame; he slept in a matter of seconds.

*

"Boy. Wake up."

Gabriel opened one eye. It was still dark and the flames in the wood burner had dwindled to pitiful embers. He could vaguely make out Seren leaning over him, the tips of her long hair brushing his nose.

"What is it? Is something wrong?"

"Nothing's wrong. Just come with me."

He turned to check on Annabel. Her mouth was open and her fingers curled; thumb still pointing upwards. She was dead to the world.

Gabriel followed Seren outside the hut. The hairs stood up on his arms and neck and he let out a little hiss of disapproval. He didn't want to be in the cold. He especially didn't want to leave Annabel.

Seren waved for him to follow as she stomped off through the long grass.

Gabriel stared towards the horizon. The green light was visible only as a slim line in the distance. Dawn was breaking, but night still reigned strong.

"Hurry!" she urged.

"I don't want to leave Annabel –"

"She'll be fine. We'll be back before she knows we've left."

"Where are we going in such a hurry?"

"Shh!" Seren came to a standstill at a wooden fence. It was tall – much taller than Gabriel – with thin gaps between each plank. On the other side there was more grass and what looked like a large farm. Seren found a plank of wood that had come loose from its rusty nails and slipped through the gap easily. When she waved her hand, Gabriel squeezed through in pursuit, only to find she was running swiftly ahead. What on earth was she doing?

"Since old farmer MacIntyre lost his good hand to the King, he hasn't been able to shoot his rifle," Seren said, as Gabriel caught up with her. His breathing was heavy – a lot heavier than hers it seemed.

In a simple wooden enclosure, chickens sat

sleepily. Gabriel had once seen a Nightcrawler breaking into a coop back home, tearing the poor critters heads off and lapping up the blood. He'd slain it before all the birds were lost. But these chickens were unconcerned by their intruders as Seren opened the door.

"Help me steal some eggs."

"What? No!"

She rounded on him. "Why not?"

"Because like you said, it's stealing."

"And what do you propose I feed you and the little one?"

"You said you had vegetables…"

"I do. But that's not the point. I like eggs." It was very dark inside, but Seren was used to the layout of the pen as she reached in and fumbled around for a prize. The chickens became irritable as she shoved them aside roughly from their beds. "Take these," she instructed, passing two eggs to Gabriel.

Sighing loudly so she could hear he wasn't entirely happy about it, he slipped the eggs in his pockets and checked that no one had seen. The sky was lightening somewhat and he could make out the gap in the wooden fence a good distance away.

A light came on in the farmhouse.

"Seren," he breathed.

"Just a few more –"

The breath caught in Gabriel's throat as a door opened and an old woman came out on the porch. She looked to the fence ahead of her, the gap in the planks a clear giveaway, then shot a look to the coop.

"Thieves!" she shrieked. "MacIntyre! Thieves in

the chicken coop again!"

The old woman disappeared inside the farmhouse in a hurry and Gabriel gripped Seren by the waist, pulling her out. Her merry eyes danced with mischief as she began running for the exit, her bare feet virtually soundless in the grass. Gabriel blundered behind her, trying to keep up. He felt his heart leap into his mouth as a shot sounded in the night. There would be no coming back from a bullet wound this time if he was hit.

"You said… he couldn't… shoot anymore!" he rasped.

Seren laughed. "I didn't say his wife couldn't!"

She was the first to reach the fence and slipped out of sight, just as another shot sounded. A hole penetrated a plank of wood inches from Gabriel's head as he rammed his body through the gap. He could feel Seren pulling on his arm on the other side and when he'd forced himself through, he tumbled to the floor. A crunch sounded in his left pocket. Yolk oozed through his trouser leg.

Seren paced around him, dancing on her tiptoes and laughing wildly. She held two eggs in each hand, twirling around until she felt sick.

"Wasn't that fun?"

"Fun?" he growled, dragging broken eggshell from his clothes and dumping it onto the floor. The egg in his other pocket had survived, just about. "That was stupid. If we'd been shot, then Annabel would have –"

"But we weren't," Seren cut in. She looked sober now.

"Still. She needs me to take care of her. It's not a

good idea to take risks."

"Wasn't coming to this Kingdom a huge risk in the first place?"

"Yes but –"

"Then what are you worrying about?"

He didn't like how nonchalant she was being about it. They could have been killed and for what? A handful of eggs. Small eggs to be precise.

No longer willing to listen to the strange woman, he started walking back to the hut; all the while, feeling her eyes on him.

Chapter 10

Seren had permitted Gabriel to sleep for another hour or so when they arrived back at the hut. It felt as if his eyes had only closed for a heartbeat before she'd unkindly prodded his side with her toes.

"Boy," she said, in an unnecessary *loud* voice.

He jumped with a start, his eyes fixed upon an axe in the young woman's delicate hands, and he raised his arms in protection.

"Get up," she said, dropping the axe to the wooden floor with a *clank* – the sharp edge of the blade narrowly missing his shoulder. "You'll need this."

Annabel stirred beside him, yawning and raising her hands above her head in a sharp stretch. "I slept like the dead," she declared, then as an afterthought added, "Good morning, Gabriel."

"I think 'good' is the wrong word for it," he mumbled, scratching his leg. He could smell the tang of sweat on his skin, lingering after all that running.

Annabel frowned and watched him climb to his feet, the axe in his grasp. He was warily watching Seren exit the hut, returning with a steaming pot. Breakfast had been prepared outside that morning.

"Eggs," she announced. "Boiled. Sit both of you."

Annabel rushed to the wooden table, hopping in joy. She clapped her hands and smiled broadly as Seren served two boiled eggs to a plate, followed by a couple of slices of bread.

"Ooh yummy. I'm starving."

"I thought you might be." Seren stared over at Gabriel as she dispatched two eggs to her own plate. She then leaned over and spooned the last two onto his, both looking remarkably smaller than the rest. But he did not verbally pass judgement. Seren was upset he hadn't enjoyed their little game at the farmhouse, he realised that. But she was being very immature about it. And to think, she'd once had a husband!

"Hmm, still yolky," Annabel chirped. "I love eggs."

"I'm glad." Seren sat down and passed a hunk of lightly toasted bread to Gabriel. He placed the axe at his feet, took it and nodded in thanks.

"What will you do today, Seren?" Annabel asked, chewing loudly.

"Take clothes to the river to wash. You can join me if you like?"

Annabel wrinkled her nose up and looked to Gabriel. She didn't like the idea of leaving him and she especially didn't like the idea of doing chores.

"Afterwards, we can visit the market again. I've never been shopping with another young lady."

"That sounds like fun," Annabel agreed, forgetting about the washing clothes part and thinking about the smell of food. "We can have a good look around this time, can't we Gabriel?"

Gabriel kept his mouth firmly shut. He didn't want Annabel out of his sight. It wasn't just that he was unsure of Seren's intentions – it was that the little one could be a real handful sometimes. But maybe some bonding woman to woman would be good for them.

Seren smiled, her eyes twinkling. "Gabriel is helping me today with something I've had a lot of trouble with on my own. I need him to cut wood for me. I'm afraid I've struggled with it and as you've probably noticed, there are very few men around with two hands to hold an axe."

"Will it take long?"

Seren shrugged, plunging a piece of bread into her egg. "Depends how fast he works. But I'm afraid, if he doesn't do it, I have no choice but to send you both on your way. Food doesn't come free."

Yeah right, Gabriel thought.

He looked up from his plate. He understood her now. The wood cutting was payment for their stay at her hut, which he felt was reasonable enough. At least she hadn't asked him to steal again.

"We have some important stuff to do–" Annabel began.

"It can wait a day or two," Gabriel cut in. "I'll cut your wood for you. But then you must let us run our own errands."

Seren nodded curtly.

"Cut me a nice pile of wood boy and you can do as you wish."

*

Annabel kissed Gabriel goodbye on the cheek as the burning sunlight, in the bizarre green sky, beat down on their backs. It was to be a glorious day and even the wheezy barks of the strange flying beasts overhead didn't deter them. Both Annabel and Gabriel had a lot on their minds. Gabriel, work. And Annabel, exploring.

Annabel gave him one last look as she entered the woods – Gabriel's axe working away at a stubborn chunk of wood – and followed after the many layers of Seren's grey swirling skirts.

Seren danced along the earth-path as she went; a brimming basket of linen in her thin arms. She sang as loud as she could, her lungs strong and her voice, beautiful.

Darkness black and daylight green,
Whispers sharp and eyes unseen –
I dance for you on grassy fronds,
And sing for you, a simple song.

Take one look, upon her face,
Marvel at her royal grace,
Sister one and sister two,
Just might be the death of you!

She chuckled after the second verse and swirled around, making Annabel uneasy. Was this song for her benefit? Or did Seren sing madly to herself always?

"I wrote that," Seren explained, as if reading Annabel's thoughts. "When my husband left me. There are a great many verses, but they become somewhat graphic and not for a child's ears." She laughed again.

Annabel did not have time to ponder over Seren's confession for long, as they suddenly came upon a vast pond. It was surrounded by flat rocks, with shimmering pools of water in their cracks and hollows. Upon the rocks sat a group of skinny women, all tending to their washing and chatting merrily.

Heads lifted as Seren approached and a few glanced to one another, lips suddenly sealed and brows furrowed – a silent disapproval it seemed. Annabel thought that perhaps it was *her* presence that caused the thickening of tension. She was a stranger after all.

"Hello ladies!" Seren sang.

The women mumbled in response. There were five altogether, dressed mainly in ragged clothes and all looking worse for wear. Their hair was unkempt and their eyes sombre. They cleaned their husband's clothes with bitter hearts, forced to carry out the days chores that their hand-less partners couldn't. When the clothes were done, they would go home and bake bread, tend to their houses, pay taxes to the King and pray deeply that things would change. Oh, how they wanted change!

"Who's the little one?" asked a woman with a rag tying her hair back from her sweaty face.

Annabel twiddled her fingers nervously.

"She's a traveller," Seren replied, dipping a grubby cream coloured gown into the water.

"A traveller? At her age?"

"She has a brother."

The woman grunted. This information was sufficient enough. They all worked on in silence, no longer interested. Annabel sat cross-legged on a rock, which was warm against her skin, and waited for Seren to scrub the clothes until the black dirt and muddy smears had come away as best they could. She was bored. She considered taking the path back home, when at last Seren dumped the soggy clothes back in their basket.

"Come on then, we'll drop these back and go to the market. See how your *brother* is getting on while we're at it."

Uplifted, Annabel skipped the rest of the way to the hut and even joined in when Seren started singing the song she'd written for her cruel, disloyal husband.

*

Gabriel wiped the sweat from his face. He could feel the sizzling pain as the flesh of his neck burned in the sunlight. Ripping off the sleeves of his shirt, he used one to tie around his neck like a scarf, to stop his skin from burning any more.

He worked quickly, sawing into the fallen tree by the hut and taking back sections to his workbench. His pile of kindling was growing and growing. He was sure that he would be finished much sooner than he'd first thought.

"Hope this is good enough for you," he said to himself, slinging two halves onto the pile, breathing heavy. He walked to a bucket and dipped his hands in, bringing the water to his lips. He'd obtained a few splinters in the soft flesh of his palms throughout the day and knew he'd be up all night, picking the blighters back out.

When his stomach grumbled in protest, he wandered into the hut in search of food. Seren's shelves were bare, besides chopped herbs in jars that looked withered and old. There was a half loaf of bread left and a small ration of dried meat in a drawstring sack that he couldn't determine its origin. He ate a little regardless. And when the aching in his gut stopped, he put the sack back where he'd found it, and swiped the bread crumbs into his palm, tipping them to the earth outside for the birds.

It wasn't long after that Annabel returned, waving her hands above her head.

"We're back!"

"I can see," Gabriel said, with a grin.

She ran to him and pressed her head to his belly, hugging him tight.

"Everything all right?" he asked.

She nodded and the butterflies of worry in his stomach stopped tickling him.

"Well, boy. You've certainly made light work of that tree," Seren said in approval. "Take a break if you want. Finish the rest tomorrow."

"If you don't mind, I'd like to carry on and get it all done."

Seren tilted her head to the side. She stared at him. "So eager to leave?"

"Eager to explore," he replied, feeling the butterflies returning.

"There's plenty of time for exploring," she

smiled. "Come on Anna'. Let's spread these clothes on the grass and let them dry." She held her hand out for Annabel, who took it without question.

Gabriel watched them both crouch down in the grass yonder, flapping wet clothes and laying them flat on the ground. It occurred to him then that his young friend wasn't complaining. She hadn't said 'no' to helping Seren and she hadn't snapped at him for not hurrying up. Could it be – Annabel had found some form of peace here?

He swung his axe and missed the block of wood in front of him, almost hitting himself in the shin with the blade.

Pay attention, he thought, his heart pounding. He dragged his eyes from the young women. *Pay attention, fool.*

Chapter 11

Annabel and Seren entered the market through some shrubbery; Annabel almost tripping over Seren's many skirts as they went. They giggled behind their hands as they tumbled out into the open, immersing themselves amongst the citizens of the Kingdom. Both girls had flowers tucked behind their ears – daisies that had let out a faint squeal when they'd been plucked from their stems.

Annabel felt for the first time that she had a friend she could actually relate to; a sister even. Gabriel was a fine companion, (murderer aside) but he wasn't a girl.

"Here," Seren said, popping a small bronze coin into Annabel's small palm. "Buy what you wish. A gift from me." She reached out and tweaked Annabel's nose, before continuing on through the crowd. Annabel stared at the coin. It displayed the face of a crowned and bearded man, looking regal and handsome in his old age. It was no doubt the King of this strange and foreign land, the one who took the hands of his country's men.

"Cheeses. Cheeses here!" cried a woman.

"Goats milk. Fresh goats milk!"

"Apples from the finest apple trees!"

"Vegetable pies! Warm and tasty!"

Annabel skipped onwards, clutching the coin to her chest. She stared at all the tables with budding enthusiasm. This time she would not have to beg to fill her belly. And if she could afford to, she'd like to bring Gabriel something. She felt sorry for him, labouring with that axe all day long.

"Honey cakes! Sweet, delicious honey cakes!"

Annabel paused and tugged on Seren's skirt. "Wait!"

"What is it child? Do you see something you like?"

An old crone held a honey cake aloft, bragging about its heavenly taste. When she spotted the wide eyes of the young girl, she lowered the cake in her gnarled hands, so Annabel could see the glazed sponge of the delightful little morsel.

"Two for a penny," the crone informed her.

"Three," Seren replied.

The old crone scowled at the young woman. "Two."

"Three," Seren repeated.

"You'll get three cakes for a penny and a half!"

"Three cakes for one penny," Seren hissed. "You know as well as I that cakes are a luxury and few buy them."

The two women locked stares. Annabel marvelled at the intensity in Seren's eyes and the sudden fear in the crone's.

"Fine. Three for a penny." She quickly handed them over and Seren nodded for Annabel to hand over the coin.

"Pleasure doing business with you," Seren said, with a hint of sarcasm.

The old crone watched them go with a weary gaze.

"Seren-" Annabel began, through a mouthful of cake.

"Yes?"

"Why is it people...well... they look at you funny?"

A smile touched the lips of the beautiful young woman, her hair longer than anyone Annabel had ever seen. It was healthy and shiny – nothing like the lank and dirty locks of the people all around them.

"They're jealous," Seren whispered, as if it were a secret, "of my good looks." She tried to keep a straight face then laughed. Annabel smiled with her. And that, it seemed, ended the subject.

A horn sounded just as Annabel was picking the last of the crumbs from the front of her dress with the tip of her finger. She looked up immediately, and wondered what danger she might be in. Suddenly, she wished Gabriel were at her side. She felt small and alone.

Again, a loud blast tore through the market, silencing everyone.

"Who is it?" whispered a boy, no older than Annabel. He tugged on the unbuttoned sleeve of a man who was rife with stubble on his prominent chin. "Is it a cursed one?"

"Hurry inside son," the man said, pushing the boy into a pub with his one good hand.

"Make way for the Prince!" came a bellow.

A distinct sigh of relief came from the surrounding people, including the man and his boy. Annabel reached towards Seren's hand. Seren was standing on the balls of her feet, eyes drawn to a copse of trees that had come alive – parting ways for a parade of fine white horses.

"Is it okay to look?" Annabel asked, straining to speak as she barely took in a breath.

"Oh yes, child. You wouldn't want to miss this!"

The people of the Kingdom bowed as three men galloped forth and then dismounted with clicks and clacks of armour. It became obvious to Annabel that the men and women were gazing upon the parade without fear or suspicion.

"Ooh!" Annabel gasped.

"I know," Seren muttered, as she curtsied respectfully with the other women.

The Prince – Delwyn as he was so christened – stood before them, his long strawberry blonde hair dancing around a perfectly chiselled face. His chin bore a hint of a manly dip in its centre and his cheekbones were high and prominent. His eyes were a crisp, unforgettable blue – a blue that could rival Gabriel's – and he was taller than most in his presence.

Delwyn nodded in greeting to the people as he passed and smiled broadly at all who acknowledged him. But what the people didn't know was that his smile was forced. Deep down, he was an unhappy young man. Life was a trial for him, day in and day out. He longed for freedom from the curse, just like everyone else under his father's rule.

"A pear, Prince Delwyn?" asked a bold teenage girl. Her eyelashes fluttered daintily as she offered the dashing young man a piece of fruit, still moist with morning dew.

"Thank you," he said, taking it from the girl's slender fingers.

She watched in awe, hoping he might take a bite before her very eyes, but when he passed it to one of his guard – standing morosely nearby – she wilted and turned to her mother, who smiled with encouragement regardless.

Delwyn walked the stretch of the market slowly and in time, the people resumed hustling and bustling, forgetting he was even there. Annabel, however, could not take her eyes off him. He was perfect! He was the one that would no doubt satisfy the wicked vampire waiting back home. She wanted to tell Gabriel at once. But Seren had other ideas.

"A fine day, Prince," she said, leaving Annabel to trail behind her. She walked with a spring in her step and her hands held behind her back.

Delwyn lifted his head and gave Seren's lean body a subtle look. He nodded in agreement, waving his guard away when they drew near for his protection. At the Prince's hip there rested a grand old sword, once wielded by his father in battle. It was encrusted with rubies and worth more than all the food and clothing at the market, put together. He had been warned by his mother of thieves at the market. He had also been warned of those who might try to win his heart for a chance to live a life of wealth at the palace.

"You look like you've suffered a lack of sleep."

Prince Delwyn blanched. Who was this girl, so boldly picking faults in his exterior? The cheek of her! But a part of him actually softened at her honesty. It was a rare thing, to be told truths in the Kingdom. Most were so afraid of what the King might do, they barely approached him.

"Tired, I guess. Nightmares."

"You're haunted by nightmares, my Prince?"

He nodded, wondering if he'd said too much.

"Might I ask, what it is you dream of?"

This was, perhaps, too personal now, he thought flinchingly.

Annabel noticed the look of discomfort on the Prince's face and waited with bated breath for Seren to move away from him. She knew very little about royalty, as there were no such thing as Prince's and King's in her world, other than the ones in story books, but she knew enough to respect them and, well, leave them be.

"Darkness," Prince Delwyn said. "The darkness that surrounds my sisters."

"Ah, it is a common thing amongst us all," Seren replied.

He glanced down at his feet. "Yes, but I should have at least been able to find the one who did this to them by now."

Seren reached out a hand and gripped the cold armour cloaking the Prince's arm – another brave gesture that alerted the guards, making them stand to attention.

"It is a sad thing, to be sure. But you'll find that

person." She took a hold of Annabel suddenly and moved light footedly away from the bewildered Prince. "Sleep well," she called, over her shoulder.

Chapter 12

That night, at the dinner table, Annabel didn't stop talking about Prince Delwyn.

"Eyes bluer than yours Gabriel!" she insisted.

"She's not wrong," Seren said, cutting an apple with a knife and gnawing loudly on the pieces.

Gabriel was nursing his blistered hands, dabbing at the blood and pus with a moist cloth. The axe had worn his skin raw and he didn't think he could stand to chop one more piece of wood if his life depended on it.

"He had a straight back, like a poll," Annabel said. "And long legs, like…like polls too!"

Seren tittered at this observation.

"And one of those bum-chins!"

Now they were all laughing.

"What?" Annabel exclaimed. She looked incredibly peeved by their reaction. "What's so funny?"

Seren rose to her feet when her giggles had died down and dragged her stool closer to Gabriel. Taking a strip of material that he'd torn from an old skirt she'd given him, she wrapped it around his hand and tied it in a knot. She did the same for the other, watching him wince as the force of tightening the knot grazed his flesh.

"I think he's perfect," Annabel blurted, hoping

Gabriel would catch on. Her eyes were wide.

"Hmm," he muttered noncommittally. He did not want the subject of perfect men to be broached while Seren was lingering.

"*You'd* marry him wouldn't you Seren?"

She blushed violently and Gabriel averted his gaze from her, pretending he didn't notice. Girls and their fairytale romances were not of any interest to the young boy.

"I guess I could give up living in my hut to have a chamber in the palace," she replied, almost evasively.

"You looked like you wanted to kiss him –"

Seren picked up the empty plates in silence and moved them to the counter. She didn't see Gabriel giving the little girl a warning look. He didn't appreciate teasing and didn't think it wise to push Seren for details; especially after the loss of her husband.

"Come on, bed time," Gabriel said.

"What? You're not the boss of me!" Annabel cried. "I'm not even tired."

"Annabel —"

"*Gabriel.*"

They stared at each other.

"We're getting up early in the morning. We've got things to do." His eyes widened now.

She slid off her chair and stomped towards the wood burner. The blankets were still strewn on the floor from the previous night. "Fine. Whatever." She made a show of swishing blankets about haphazardly, then thumped to the floor, almost painfully so.

"A little wine?" Seren asked, after they'd watched

Annabel's little chest rising and falling until she appeared to have settled.

"No. I'm fine thank you."

"Suit yourself," Seren muttered, and guzzled some of the liquid from a glass bottle she'd been storing away, for when the occasion called.

Gabriel fiddled idly with his bandages, wondering what to say. Just as he decided he would retire also, Seren sank onto the stool next to him.

"So I'm dying to know," she began, "why you're here. You've got nothing but the clothes on your backs after all. Come on. You can tell me." She gave him her most trusting look.

Gabriel sighed. "We're looking for someone, for a friend of mine. That's all."

She raised her eyebrows a little. "Who?"

"That's between me and Annabel," he said, uncomfortably.

"Oh, is it now?"

He nodded and scratched at a patch of dried mud on one elbow.

"Secrets. So many secrets." She waved the wine melodramatically and a splash of red liquid landed on her skirt.

Gabriel eyed it. It resembled a splatter of blood.

"We wouldn't be human if we didn't have them," he said quietly, more to himself than her.

"Right you are." She lifted the bottle to her lips and took another mouthful. It wasn't long before Gabriel bid her goodnight.

*

Prince Delwyn paced his chambers – situated in the east wing of the palace – feeling irritable and as always, morbidly depressed. In his hand was the pear from the market-girl, which he tossed up and down, deep in thought.

The reds and golds of his bedroom's décor seemed all the more richer this evening. Someone had cleaned during his venture into the market. He had been lucky to get out at all that day. His sister, Floriana, had been spoiling for another hunting trip in the woods. But his father had supported *him* for a change, making it quite clear his only son needed to stretch his legs outside the grounds for some non-restricted Kingdom air.

It was all Prince Delwyn was permitted to do on escaping the grounds; a short visit to the festering filth of his father's unhappy people. All of them watching in wide eyed wonderment as he browsed. As if he were their Messiah. Their saviour. But he was beginning to think no one could save them. He'd tried so many times now, and failed so many more.

The sight of handless men tugged on his heart-strings and he rubbed at his wrists self-consciously now, pear still in hand. Rather than focusing his ungodly rage on the witch that had caused this despair and destruction, his father let it all out on his own men! Was that any way to run a Kingdom?

Things will be so very different when I rule, he thought and threw the pear at the far wall, which had been adorned with deer heads. The pear smashed into little pieces and left a slimy mark against the fancy wallpaper, bits falling on the carpet below.

Delwyn moved over to the fireplace, which was warm with the heat of golden flames. From the mantel, he plucked a framed photograph of his sisters. They were so young in this picture, holding hands and waving to the camera. When Delwyn was a boy, he'd played with them by the fountain in their grand garden. They'd dig around in the earth for worms and then drop them into the fountains cool waters, watching as they wriggled. His sisters would giggle and squawk and splash water in his face.

Their mother had been a real beauty; a woman fit for a crown he'd always thought. She'd lay regally on a chaise long with a glass of red wine in one jewelled hand. She would laugh the most delicate and heavenly laugh – before illness took her.

Prince Delwyn choked back tears. The size of the hole in his chest was expanding at the thought of all this loss. He was afraid of being alone. He was afraid of being like his father, who barely spoke two words to him on a weekly basis. The King was too concerned with private matters. Instead of sharing them with his boy, he locked himself away, either in the throne room or his bed chambers. And his favourite thing to tell his nineteen year old boy was, 'you're a man now. You don't need me.'

He was wrong.

Prince Delwyn lowered the picture frame to the marble mantle. Pain was heavy in his chest, screaming for an outlet, but he wasn't going to give it one. Prince's don't cry – that was another of his father's favourite things to say.

"Where is she?" he seethed. He kicked the glass coffee table, knocking over two gold candle sticks that sputtered and flickered out. He thought of the witch, hiding someplace out of reach. She may have travelled too far out of reach by now. But one thing he knew was that she was still alive; only when a witch was dead would all her curses on mankind lift.

*

"You're positive you haven't told Seren why we're here, right?"

Gabriel and Annabel were walking along an unfamiliar lane, which according to Seren would take them along the border of the Kingdom, whilst skirting the forest. They had left the hut under the pretence they were going exploring and that they would join Seren for their evening meal on their return.

"No, I did not," Annabel huffed, pulling at squealing flower heads as she went. "You don't trust me at all, do you?"

The wheezy barks of the strange winged beasts of this land came from the treetops. They were warning calls; informing humans to stay away from their territory.

"Let's go back to the market."

"Why?" Gabriel sneered, "So you can get distracted by honey cakes and handsome Princes?"

Annabel glowered at him but said nothing,

ripping more forcefully at the flowers. It wasn't until one of the flowers bit her with tiny teeth that she kept her hands at her sides.

They strolled along vast farmlands, with crops that had long since wilted. Women tended to them, watering dull green pea pods and the large, browning husks of sweetcorn. They harvested wheat and sowed seeds, all of them wiping their brows at intervals with grubby cloths.

"You know, she's not so bad," Annabel piped up, when they'd passed a cow with two tails, beating at giant black flies near its rear end.

"I assume we're talking about Seren?"

"Hmm."

"We barely know her –"

"I think she's nice." Annabel thought about the little bronze coin that had paid for the cakes. Laughing loudly, they had both split the third cake on the way home, having decided that Gabriel would be better off without the sweet taste of honey in his parched mouth. They didn't want him to get podgy after all!

"She'd probably help if you asked her. It would make things so much easier."

"We don't need help."

"I'm only say-*ing*." She exaggerated her words moodily.

They came upon a small cottage, with bright blooming flowers tittering and whistling in the green sunlight. Seren had warned them of bad weather, but it had been a clear crisp day so far.

With their feet crunching under the small gravel,

Gabriel and Annabel approached the small iron gate. When he stopped, Annabel accidentally ploughed in to the back of him. She rubbed her forehead and frowned grumpily.

An old woman stood on the wooden porch yonder, her spine awkwardly bent. She was sweeping, though her bad back appeared to be a mighty hindrance. But she was determined to disperse the dust and mud. She lifted her head when she heard the squeak of the gate hinges and with her sudden curiosity came the appearance of a young man at the front door behind her. He looked to be in his thirties, tall and strong. His hair was a sandy blonde colour, shoulder length and tied back with a ribbon. He squinted at the two faces peering over the front gate and placed a hand on the old woman's back. To Gabriel's surprise, the man had both hands.

"Hello," Gabriel said. "One of the lucky ones too I take it?"

"I'm sorry?"

"Your hands. You have both."

"Oh. Yes, I do." He looked at them like he'd just noticed they were his.

"Tell them to leave," the old woman croaked. "We don't like strangers around these parts."

The man nodded in response.

"You heard her. No strangers."

Gabriel felt desperation pool in his innards like ice water.

"Please, I won't take up too much of your time."

"Is something wrong with your ears?" the woman rasped, leaning against her broom for support. "Go away now."

"But Sir –"

"It's Daniel," the man said with a sigh.

"Daniel. May I ask you something...kind of...er...personal?"

The young man looked thoroughly interested suddenly, but glanced at the old woman as if to make sure it was safe to continue. She rolled her eyes at him and began sweeping once more. Daniel, feeling somewhat braver, stepped from the porch onto the little path leading to the gate.

"What is it?" he sighed. "Be quick. I do not like to linger outside when there could be Princesses about."

"Do you, by any chance, seek a wife?" Gabriel persevered.

Daniel let out a loud guffaw, which startled the old woman into ceasing mid sweep. "I guess you haven't put two and two together," he said. "I'm already happily married. To her." He pointed over his shoulder and the old woman smiled smugly at the two astonished strangers.

"So on your way!" she cackled.

"Are you seri -?" Gabriel clapped a hand over Annabel's mouth and dragged her away down the lane before she could finish her sentence. When the cottage was a good distance behind them, he freed her.

"She was old enough to be his granny," she spat.

"Each to their own," he replied, slightly disturbed by the prospect of marrying one so 'over the hill.'

Annabel couldn't fathom why any handsome man would want to marry an ugly old woman who could barely stand up straight. It was ludicrous. But on the other hand, why would anyone want to marry a shape shifting, evil vampire?

"We need help," she whined again.

"No we don't. We've got time –"

"We've got nothing, Gabriel."

Suddenly, the earth vibrated beneath their feet. A thundering, rumbling noise sounded and Annabel looked to Gabriel for an explanation. Gabriel knew what it was of course. It was all too familiar to him. His mind was taken back to a time when villagers had caught him draining the blood of a shire horse. He hadn't killed the beast, he'd merely drained enough to put it into a gentle sleep. The horse would have woken with aches and pains, but it would have lived. But as Gabriel lay in the filthy, manure encrusted hay, digesting his intake, a stable boy had found him there all covered in blood. The alarm had been sounded before the vampire could silence the lad. Twelve men on horses, bearing flaming torches, had chased him into the mountains on a full stomach where he'd stayed hidden for a fortnight, much to Annabel's irritation. For a while, he'd feared a second death.

"Get off the road."

Annabel didn't need telling twice. Together they rushed under the cover of the dense and leafy canopy, where the trees moved lazily without the aid of wind. As they watched cautiously from behind a prickly bush with yellow buds, a small army tore passed at high speed.

Gabriel felt a pang of fear. Were they looking for him? Had the Princess been out hunting for a boy with two hands? He sincerely hoped he'd never find out.

Chapter 13

"Your father has sent word," a short, weathered female said at the grand oak door of Prince Delwyn's chambers. Her name eluded his memory.

"Speak," he urged her, showing interest in a spider crawling along his door frame.

The maid didn't hesitate.

"The Princesses are currently dining in the garden and will be practising their archery in the orchard after brunch. They won't be entering the palace until you send word you've returned safely to your quarters."

He smiled. "Thank you."

She curtsied low in her long purple gown – the King's colour – and her many skirts touched the floor. As she made to leave, another maid approached, much younger than she and as thin as a broom.

"My Prince," she said, performing a neat curtsy of her own. "Your army has returned. They have sent for you."

Delwyn felt his chest flutter with both excitement and angst. At last, some news – and at such a convenient time! He pushed passed the maids in a hurry, buttoning up a silver coloured waistcoat over his crisp white shirt as he went, vaguely aware that they were following behind him. They eventually disappeared down a narrow flight of stairs that led to the underbelly of the castle. These were the servants' quarters, where they sowed clothing, gossiped and slept on dusty cots. It was no better than the dungeons, Delwyn had heard, but he had never ventured down there to see for himself.

In the vast courtyard, alight with sunshine, he found his knights. On his arrival, they knelt awkwardly in their armour.

"Rise," he commanded.

They did so.

"What news, Elanor? Did you find her?"

They'd been gone for so many weeks now, it seemed hard to believe they'd returned at all. Elanor had led the women into an un-named region of wasteland, then into the mountains that they had spied with a telescope from the tallest tower of the palace. Elanor, the strongest of the Prince's knights, had sworn she'd seen a singular trail of smoke rising from the trees on cold days. It had to be the witch in hiding, surely.

"We tracked down the source of the recent fires and found a small hut in the mountains. We surrounded it and Bethan took lead. She was hit in the chest with a curse that made her skin melt from her very bones!"

The knights were silent and still, looking pained by the memory of a lost comrade. Delwyn opened his mouth in surprise.

"Sasha then set the hut aflame," Elanor continued, "which brought the witch running out in a panic. I nailed her with an arrow in the heart and have brought you her head." She bowed and gestured for one of the knights to step forward. A dark haired woman with almond eyes and thick, exotic eyelashes dropped a sack on the floor.

Delwyn raised his head in astonishment, fixing his gaze on Elanor, whose eyes were twinkling with expectation. He knelt and parted the neck of the sack, gasping at the sight of a fly infested face. He placed the crook of his arm to his nose so as not to intake the putrid smell that came from the old witch.

What was he feeling now? Fear? Relief? Pity even? Was it truly over? Could he finally look upon his sisters faces; sit in the grounds and laugh with them as the dogs chased their tails and whilst the King's fool pranced and danced?

When a witch is killed, all curses performed in her wretched life are lifted. If this truly was the head of the witch who had caused his family so much distress, then at last, there would be no more magic to haunt their Kingdom.

"Test them," Delwyn instructed.

"My Prince?"

"You know what I've asked of you," he barked.

The women looked nervously at their leader and then knelt once more. "Yes, Sir!" they cried in unison.

*

Gabriel was thirsty. It seemed so long since he'd drained a cup of water and his mouth was so dry, he could barely shift his tongue.

"I'm fed up," Annabel groaned. "We've been

walking for hours."

She wasn't exaggerating either. They'd stopped at every hut, cottage and house asking worthy men if they would take the hand of a mysterious woman 'back home.' It was on the nineteenth refusal that Gabriel was beginning to realise that honesty was going to achieve nothing.

"We have to lie to them," Annabel said, as if reading his mind. "We have to make up a lie and get someone to come home with us. It's the only way."

"Like what?"

She shrugged. "Tell them they can marry me."

He smiled, his lips cracking as he did so. "You may feel like your hundreds of years old, little one, but to the naked eye, you're eight years old."

"So? If men here can marry Granny's, I'm sure there will be someone willing to marry a child too."

She had a point.

"I wouldn't want to risk you getting hurt."

"Too late for that."

They walked in peace for a short length, admiring the palace as it drew closer into range. It had many turrets and windows, and was built of sturdy grey stone. On the towers, there fluttered purple flags sporting pictures of a green sun.

"Ask Seren," Annabel suggested suddenly.

"No."

"She might know someone."

"No."

"Well if that *freak* comes and gets us for failing her, I'm going to be *so* angry with you, I think I might explode."

"I don't doubt that," he told her.

When the stone walls of the palace increased in definition, Gabriel admitted defeat. He did not wish to get too close, in case a Princess spotted him from a window. He knew perfectly well that there would be no chance of charming his way out of any given situation involving one of them.

The walk back to Seren's hut felt like the longest journey of their lives. Slowly they made their way along the lane, passing some familiar disgruntled faces. Rain began to fall, drenching them from head to toe and it was a small victory when they made it back before the thunder shook the skies and lightning hit with a fierce energy.

"Empty handed," Seren commented as they shook the rain from their hair like dogs. "I take it you didn't find what you were looking for?"

Gabriel quietly took off his boots and left them by the door, next to Annabel's little shoes. He watched her peel off her white socks and noticed the blisters all over her feet.

"Why didn't you tell me?" he asked, his face full of concern.

She draped the socks over a chair. "What use would it have been? You wouldn't have listened."

Gabriel closed his eyes for a second and inhaled sharply. "Annabel, I'm not sure you quite understand how much I care about you."

Seren wandered over with two towels, which she handed to her dripping guests. She then returned to her counter to chop tomatoes for a salad without a word.

"Annabel," Gabriel persisted. "Are you listening?"

"All right. Yes, I heard you. You care about me."

"If your feet were bleeding, you should have said something."

"I know."

"Then why didn't you?"

She towelled her hair dry, keeping her focus on that instead of Gabriel's stern expression. "Because I wanted to be strong, like you."

His chest deflated as the breath he'd been holding escaped loudly through his lips.

"You're the toughest eight year old I've ever met," he said. "But a human should know their limits. We're not dead anymore."

Annabel shot a look at Seren, and Gabriel flushed red. He was so caught up in the moment, he forgot she was nearby. But it appeared she hadn't heard them.

"Let's dry off by the fire," he said.

She nodded and followed him to their nest of blankets. Seren, suspiciously quiet, served them plates of lettuce, tomatoes, cucumber and beetroot drizzled with balsamic oil, which they ate in their makeshift beds. Seren sat cross-legged beside them on the wooden floor, her gaze distant as she watched the flames eating the wood logs Gabriel had prepared.

"You can stay with Seren tomorrow," Gabriel said, having swallowed the last bite of his salad. "If she doesn't mind."

"I should start charging you extra for minding the

child," Seren replied with a mischievous grin. She dutifully took his plate and piled it on top of her own.

"I'm not a baby," Annabel declared.

"No, you're right, child. But still, there are strange people about. You wouldn't want to be alone in this land."

Annabel didn't feel like arguing. She yawned and curled up beside Gabriel, who moved his hand to her golden hair. It had dried in wavey lines. Gently, he stroked it.

"Tomorrow will be a better day," he promised. "I can feel it in my bones."

*

"A thief, my Prince," Elanor announced. She and another of the knight's in armour had a firm hold on a scrawny, bedraggled young man with more than a day's stubble growth. He looked dirty and wild as he pulled against the two women sandwiching him.

"Please, no! Don't!"

"He has no hands at all," Delwyn pointed out. "How can a hand-less man be a thief?"

"You'd be surprised what thieves can do. He scares sheep from one field to the next and marks them as his own with paint."

Delwyn thought about this. If a man who already had no hands was placed under a curse, his father would execute him. There was no mercy the third time around.

"Make way for the King!" came a feminine cry

from a tower.

In swooping, elegant robes of amethyst and gold, the King himself entered the courtyard. Upon his head of snowy white hair sat a jewel encrusted crown and in his hand, a golden staff. When he'd been a young and blood thirsty warrior, leading armies to war and back, he had suffered an injury to his leg. It had grown infected and was on the brink of severance, until signs of recovery became apparent. Now, he hobbled wherever he went.

"Father," Delwyn greeted, bowing his head.

"What is it you want Delwyn?"

Delwyn swallowed and indicated the sack at his feet. "My knights returned to us yesterday, father. They bring the head of a witch."

The King laughed a deep, rumbling laugh. But it was not from merriment. He had heard this story before. Many villagers had brought heads to his throne room, claiming to have killed the witch; hoping for riches in return for their bravery. His son, of course, did not desire payment in gold. He wanted payment in freedom.

"Let's see then," he said, deciding to humour him. He peered into the sack and recoiled at the sight of big fat house flies buzzing around a pale face. "And this man is to be your sacrifice?"

The thief, who had been quiet in the King's presence, began writhing and wriggling again. "No! No please! Not this!"

The King cut a look at his son, who was standing patiently before him straight as a rod.

"Indulge me, Father," he begged. "The curse may have lifted at last."

"Of course, of course," the King said, patting Delwyn between his shoulder blades. The King clicked his fingers. A maid, who had been hiding behind the King's trailing robes with her hands neatly folded in front of her, pulled two strips of silk cloth from her pinafore.

"Elanor, Sasha, be witness. Miriam, send for my sister Rosemary," the Prince commanded as the King's maid advanced on him. He lowered his head so she could reach, tying the scarf about his eyes and careful not to catch his hair in the knot at the back. The King was next, though he was shorter than his son and did not need to sink any lower than he already was.

"Thank you, Emily," Delwyn said, for he was now completely blinded from the world. He sensed his father at his shoulder, and stood still in wait.

"How have you been anyway, my boy?" the King asked. "Truthfully."

Delwyn sighed. His father could always tell when he was lying. "Disheartened as always. Until now."

The King grunted and said nothing more on the matter. He was not a man for sharing feelings, but as a father, he felt obliged to ask.

"Please, no!" the thief howled. "I won't look! I won't!"

Elanor kicked his legs brutally from beneath him and the thief hit the ground on his knees. Sasha forced his head down, one hand on his scalp and the other on his arm.

"Princess Rosemary has arrived," Emily kindly informed them and an air of unease rippled amongst the men.

Rosemary was nothing like her horrid sister, Floriana. She was kind and beautiful, with a swanlike neck and not a single pit or scar on her face. She had eyes like her brother – a blue that shone with inner light – and skin as pale as moonlight. Her brown hair was long and braided neatly down her back, laced with emerald ribbons. And upon her head, there rested a string of tiny daisies that she'd been linking together in the garden before her summons.

"Father," she said, kissing him gently on his wrinkled cheek. "Brother." She kissed the Prince, standing on the tiptoes of her golden slippers.

Her dress was green and gold, adorned with patterns of ivy along its sleeves. It fitted snugly about the curves of her body that had started to form in recent years. She was becoming a woman and it hurt her that her own father could not see how much she'd grown.

The thief whined as if in pain. He kept his head down and his eyes firmly shut.

"My darling Rosemary," the King smiled. "You smell wonderful dear."

"I was sat in the flowers, Father."

"I know child. You're like mother nature herself." He did not know if he was smiling directly at her, but he did so regardless.

"Rosemary," Delwyn began, excitement building within him. "I think my knights may have found the witch."

"Really?" she breathed in delight.

"We aren't entirely positive. But we have high

hopes," he added.

Elanor and Sasha nodded in agreement.

"Would you do me the honour of looking into the eyes of this thief?"

The Princess looked at the desperately flailing man at her feet. She hated forcing her curse on her people. And secretly, she despised her father. For all the polite and kind words she savoured for their scheduled conversations – whilst he sat on his throne blindfolded – she felt the utmost disgust for the way he ruled the Kingdom. He was lazy after all, leaving it to her poor brother to hunt down the witch whenever he was permitted leave. Or for the knights to face treacherous missions that rarely brought results. Her brother deserved better. And so did her people.

"Fine. Lift his head."

Elanor yanked the man's head back by his hair and he squealed in pain.

"Open your eyes," she whispered, crouching down before him.

"No! I won't, Devil!"

Rosemary bit her lip. She detested vile name-calling.

"Open your eyes, in the name of the King."

"To hell with the King!" he yelled and spat at Elanor's feet.

Elanor gripped the man tighter whilst Sasha stooped down. She pried the man's left eyelid open, until his wild eye fixed upon the enchanting blue iris of the Princess. Instantly, he mellowed. All the tension in his arms and legs dissolved and he smiled back at her droopily; embracing the flurry of a working curse in his belly.

"Princess," he sighed, in adoration. "Sweet angel, mine. How honoured I am to look at your soft face."

Delwyn clenched his fists.

"You brought me the wrong witch!" he exclaimed in anger.

Elanor and Sasha looked both worried and disappointed, but the Prince could not see their reaction from beneath his blindfold.

Another failure.

The thief writhed suddenly. "Release me. Please let me free. Oh, if I do not touch her divinity I will implode! I will...I will scream until my lungs burst. Please, you must," he begged.

Rosemary wrinkled her nose in disgust and pulled away. "If you don't mind, Father. I'll go back to the garden."

"As you wish, my Rose," The King sighed. There was little else he could say on the matter. But he would not see Prince Delwyn lose hope. Sometimes, that was the only thing he found amusement in – the rising hopes and dreams of his only son.

"I'll join you," the King called after her.

Rosemary stopped and found the crook of her father's arm, linking it with her own. Still blindfolded, he allowed her to guide him inside.

"No! Don't leave!" the thief wailed. "Oh please come back. PLEASE!" Tears poured from his eyes. "I love you. I love you with every beat of my heart. Take my soul Princess! Take it with you! I'm yours. I'M

YOURS!"

Elanor looked to Sasha. Then both women looked at their Prince, who was turning in aggravated circles, still blind to the world. The maid, Emily, stood awkwardly by.

"Son," the King said, turning back to him.

"Yes, Father?"

"Execute the thief."

Misery settled inside him once more. "Yes, Father."

Chapter 14

Gabriel stood in the market, yet again, and felt all his enthusiasm trickling into non-existence. He no longer cared whom he offended, or who thought him strange. He asked every man of reasonable age and appearance if they were in search of a wife. Men grunted and groaned at him, swatted and spat. Some even drew knives from their belts to scare him off.

"Why don't *you* marry her?" a blacksmith heckled.

Gabriel scratched the back of his head nervously and backed away. The way things were going, he just might have to.

"I'll do it," a boy called to him. He stood beside a trough of water with a fat pig on a lead that was burying its snout in the dirty liquid. "My mother's dead. So's me father. No siblings to speak of. Just me and my pig. I could do with a wife."

Gabriel couldn't believe his luck. He assessed the boy; strong upper body as far as he could tell, healthy head of dark hair, good looking, thick eyebrows over brown eyes.

"You'll travel with me? To meet her?"

"Sure thing! If she's got her own house, all the

better!"

"How old are you, if you don't mind me asking?"

"Fifteen."

Gabriel's chest deflated. He was but a boy! "You're too young I'm afraid."

"Most boys marry at sixteen. I'm almost old enough."

"That may be so, but she is *much* older than you, lad."

"Can she cook, clean and perform other wifely duties?"

Gabriel pictured the strange, morphing face of his maker and the way her cloak immitated smoke. Then, he imagined her washing dishes and scrubbing clothes by a lake, a wicked smile cutting a thin sliver against her deathly pale skin.

"She's not your type."

The boy tied his pig to a wooden post and pulled his baggy trousers up higher around his waist. They were grubby, with manure on the legs. Gabriel could smell the all-too familiar odour coming from them.

""From the way you've been harping on around this place, you've got no other options but me, my friend."

Gabriel glanced around. Women with baskets and scarves tied about their hair to protect themselves from the drizzling rain, were eyeing him with interest as they passed. Word had got around about his endeavour and people were becoming suspicious.

"Believe me. She is not your type," he repeated firmly.

The boy waved his hand in bitter defeat and trudged back to his pig, which had slumped to the ground in a puddle of mud.

I give up, Gabriel thought. *I damn well give up. It's over. Let her do with me as she wishes. No one is going to fall for this 'wife' story.* He stomped back through the market, disappointed and enraged. He was in a state of disarray, full of 'what ifs' and 'maybes.' He could also sense the shivers of unease coming from the people around him.

"The Princess!" people hissed, as if it were a vicious game of who can spread the word fastest.

Men made themselves scarce and the women darted their eyes this way and that, trying to catch a glimpse of her.

Gabriel jumped from the path to a gap between two tables selling items made from cowhide. Bags, boots and belts were the last thing he saw before he clamped his lids shut.

Whispers of 'Princess' continued to ripple all around him.

But where was she?

When an aching silence descended, Gabriel prayed that it was not who he thought it was -

"Well, well! Looky what I found."

The husky tones of Princess Floriana sent adrenaline spiralling out of control through Gabriel's body. The urge to retreat almost overpowered him, but he knew if he sneaked a peak for an exit, he would end up in worse trouble.

"So the pretty one has returned."

Floriana and her two female guards approached Gabriel. She wore riding gear, with boots covered in mud and grime from an unfortunate dismount that very morning at the stables. In her haste to find the boy with midnight hair, she'd ignored her sister's suggestion of changing into something 'girly' and had gone hunting. Of course, this was a different kind of hunt entirely.

"Rise, Caleb," she ordered, touching Gabriel's chin. "You'll walk with me back to the palace. Come come."

Gabriel thought he might hyperventilate. What should he do? What *could* he do?

"My wife is expecting me," he lied quickly.

"Your wife?" she scoffed, but she sounded unsure.

"Yes. I was married. Yesterday."

"You're lying to me."

"No. I swear it. I can take you to her."

The Princess looked sceptically at Gabriel for a moment, then turned to the nearest group of women, lingering in view of the conversation. "Tell me, ladies. Have you seen this boy with a woman?"

They mumbled amongst themselves, shaking their heads.

"You know where we could go, that's even closer," she said. "The church. We could ask Reverend Stanton himself if he's married any of my father's people recently."

Gabriel blushed red.

"See, I can tell, even with your eyes closed that you're trying to make a fool of me."

"I'm not."

She made a little noise like a childish 'humph.'

"Because I rather like you, Caleb, I'll give you one last chance to be honest with me."

Heat rose up his neck and into the tips of his ears.

"Are. You. *Married?*"

"Yes."

"Then where's your ring?"

He gulped.

"Bring him," the Princess snapped and immediately her guard advanced. Gabriel was dragged to his feet. He wisely cooperated.

*

"I wish to speak with my father," Floriana declared at the entrance to her father's throne room. "Is he in there?"

"He is, Princess," the maid curtsied and opened the great, decorative doors a fraction. She squeezed through the gap, pulling a silk sash as she went. When the doors were opened to their full potential, Floriana marched forth, trailing mud along the shiny floor.

Gabriel was being dragged through behind her, two amour clad guards gripping onto his arms tightly as if he might resist at any moment. He kept his eyes shut, so there was no way he could have walked without aid.

"Father! I have a request to make."

The King was sat upon a golden throne; with plush purple cushions and lions heads carved on the arm rests. His crown had been knocked askew when the silk sash had been tied hastily around his eyes, but no one in the room felt like telling him. Somehow, it made him seem less of a threat.

Floriana didn't bother to bow or curtsy in respect as she knew well enough he couldn't see her doing it.

"I have with me a young man."

"Has he been cursed?" the King demanded gruffly.

"No. Not quite. But I admit, Father, he's rather bewitched me."

A pregnant silence fell over the room.

The King scratched his thick white moustache. He hated it when Floriana came to him with such silly musings.

Gabriel felt his palms and forehead perspire and the beat of his heart reached a catatonic speed.

"I'd like to spend some time with him, in the palace."

"There are plenty of things for you to play with. If you are bored, perhaps another puppy?"

She stamped her foot. "No. I want *him*."

"I will not have a boy endangering my daughter. If he stays in your company he will eventually see you and he will have to be disposed of!"

"I promise I won't remove his blindfold." *Until I'm ready to*, she thought wickedly.

"No!" the King bellowed; his great, deep voice ricocheting off the pillars that held the vast ceiling aloft.

"I hate you," the Princess spat and stormed away, waving sharply at her guard to follow.

When the maid at the exit closed the door behind them, Floriana swivelled quickly on the balls of her feet and faced Gabriel with her hands planted on her hips.

"I don't care what my father says, he's staying with me." She ruffled Gabriel's midnight hair.

Her guard stood silently, keeping any opinions on the matter to themselves (as they'd been instructed to). When the Princess wanted something, she had it. Wasn't that the whole point of being part of a royal family? If she didn't get what she wanted, she might as well be a beggar.

"If he happens to announce a visit, Caleb, I must insist on you holding your tongue. If you defy me, I shall have no qualms in slicing it off so that you may never speak again."

Gabriel said nothing. He was too panicked to respond.

"Take him to my bed chambers. I must speak with my sister first. Caleb, I'll be with you shortly." She sneered the last part.

Gabriel bit his tongue. He wanted to scream for help. He wanted the King to burst through the doors of his throne-room and strike his daughter in the face for failing to follow orders. *Oh Annabel*, he thought miserably. *If only we were dead still. We'd have gone from here days ago!*

What would the little girl think if he did not return? Would she believe he'd left her, like she'd said he would before their journey through the mirror had begun? Would she go home without him? And what would his maker do to her when she found she'd returned home empty handed?

Chapter 15

Floriana found her sister in the greenhouse, simpering around the tomatoes with a watering can. The youngest Princess believed whole heartedly that this was maids work and that there were many other things a princess could be doing besides talking to vegetables as if they had feelings, or ears for that matter.

"Good afternoon," Rosemary smiled warmly, placing the watering can in the hands of an awaiting maid. The maid bowed and backed away with it in hand.

"Come outside. The heat in here is unbearable," Floriana complained, touching the back of her neck. Sweat was breaking through her skin there, making the hair at her nape feel damp with grease. The only kind of sweat she welcomed was the kind she developed during a hunt; the kind of sweat that seemed worth the trouble, when she took home a prize.

Rosemary linked arms with her sister and together they left the stifling warmth of the greenhouse into the cool breeze of day.

"Is everything all right?"

Floriana stopped and let go of Rosemary's arm.

"I've brought a boy into my chambers without our father's blessing."

"You did what?!" she cried.

Floriana frowned and in a voice laden in ice said, "Keep your voice down."

"Why would you do that? Don't you remember what happened the last time? For crying out loud, Flo'."

"We all learn from our mistakes," Floriana retorted astutely.

"So they say, though *you* clearly haven't. This will all end in tragedy. Do you want to be blamed for another innocent boy's death?"

"Last time, I didn't bother telling father that there was a boy in our room and he took it out on him instead of punishing me. This time, he knows."

"Yes, but didn't you just say -"

"He didn't agree with it, I know. But we're older now. Wiser. What harm could it do me to have a little fun?"

Rosemary bit her lip.

"Why must you insist on making life so difficult for everyone?"

"Difficult?!" Floriana snapped, breaking her hushed tones and scattering the birds from their trees. "Don't tell me you haven't craved the company of a boy? Someone who doesn't want to talk about hair and dresses all day long? Someone to tell you what it is to be in love?"

"How do you know he's been in love?"

"I don't. But he will be by time I'm through."

"Flo'!" she gasped. "You're not going to *intentionally* make him fall for you, are you?"

Floriana crossed her arms over her chest. "I'm not

going to kiss and tell, sis'."

"Don't do it!" Rosemary grabbed her sister's arm as she made to leave. "It's wrong."

But what Rosemary didn't know was that in the woods, where Floriana often hunted game, she had come across many men and boys in her time. She had forced many to look at her and love her so wildly and all-consumingly that they had clawed at the walls of the palace in desperation to touch her. The males of her father's kingdom didn't have the King to blame, they only had his daughter; the one who enjoyed seeing hands hit the flagstones bloodily. All she had to do was form an expression of innocence and say 'They looked at me, father. I told them not to, but they couldn't stop themselves. I'm so sorry it came to this.'

"I'll be in my room. Don't disturb me," she growled.

"Flo,' please, reconsider-"

"And don't you *dare* tell on me, or so help me Rose', I'll never speak to you again."

Rosemary froze and watched her sister - a year younger than herself though you wouldn't think so with the authority she exhumed - march towards the palace with a familiar determination.

*

"It's getting awfully late," Annabel pointed out. She'd been standing by the open door of the hut, watching Seren stir stew over a fire outside in the fading light of day. "He should be back by now."

Seren's spoon circled rhythmically in the mixture

of rabbit meat and vegetables. She had just been thinking the same thing. "He'll be fine," she assured her in as casual a tone as she could muster.

Annabel wasn't convinced.

"Maybe we should go and find him?"

"As heroic as that would be, little one, I don't much like to leave the safety of my home after dark. The men you see, can be as beastly as the critters in the woods."

"I'm sure if we took weapons we could clobber a few one-handed or no-handed men," she scoffed.

Seren smiled. "You have a brave soul. But never the less, I won't go. Have you ever heard of the wolfman?"

"No."

Seren frowned, "What tales did they tell you from your village exactly? You know so little -"

"I wasn't much of a listener," Annabel replied in avoidance.

Seren lowered her gaze to the stew, talking as she stirred. "A wolfman is half man, half dog. There was once a wolfman that stalked about our kingdom, years ago. He killed cattle at first, but it didn't sate his thirst. So he started killing women and children while the men drank ale unknowingly. The village eventually cried out for a hero. Prince Delwyn took an army with him into the woods and slayed the beast against his father's orders-"

"Why did his father say he couldn't kill it?" Annabel cut in.

She shrugged. "Perhaps he hoped the wolfman would kill the witch that cursed his daughters. Or maybe just to protect him from possible harm. Who knows? But from the day the Prince brought the head of the wolfman to the palace, he's been forbidden from hunting with his knights outside palace grounds."

"So why are you afraid of a wolfman if he's already dead?"

Seren looked up. "Because who's to say there aren't more waiting for their revenge?"

Annabel shuddered. She stared up at the pale moon and listened to the sound of the nearby trees and reeds rustling.

"I hope he's okay."

"He's probably drinking with the rest of them."

Annabel shook her head. "Gabriel isn't one for drinking."

"The majority of men here may be miserable, but give them a pint and they'll soon come alive. They have a strong influence on others too."

Annabel pictured Gabriel clinking glasses with a handsome young man, who had been willing to step up and take the hand of Gabriel's maker back home, in their world. *They're celebrating, that's all,* she told herself.

"Come home, Gabriel," she whispered. "Come home."

*

Princess Floriana took a red scarf from her wardrobe and draped it around Gabriel's shoulders playfully. She giggled as he rocked on his knees at the foot of her bed. Her four-poster-bed was grand in design, as was all the furniture in the palace. For the most part, it was covered in the softest pillows known to man.

Her room was adorned in bronze candle brackets shaped like mer-men or mermaids with scaly tails and on the floor was a bear hide rug with black, beady eyes that stared vacantly at the wall.

A pink-feathered bird with a petite yellow beak twittered away in a cage on the balcony outside and the curtains fluttered in the breeze.

"Why are you shaking Caleb? Are you cold? I can shut the windows if you wish?"

He didn't answer.

"Or maybe this will help?" She circled him and from behind, laced her arms around his chest, whilst kneeling on the floor. When she'd hugged him long enough, she tied the scarf around his eyes and secured the knot hard so that his head jerked painfully back.

"There. You're safe for now."

The Princess began pacing her room, swinging from a bedpost with one hand and then bouncing onto the mattress.

"Lay here with me, Caleb."

Gabriel obediently rose to his feet and heard the Princess's laughter as he felt blindly for her bed. When his fingers came across the silk touch of her covers, he crawled gently on and sat cross-legged, with no idea which way he faced.

A head found his lap. Floriana rested there so that she might feel the warmth of his leg against her oily skin.

"Tell me all about yourself. Leave nothing out."

"Everything?" he asked, thinking about his dark history. If he told her he once ate a child to survive, would she still rest her head so lovingly on his thigh?

"Yes. It's not hard," she said, with a feisty air.

"Um... well... I grew up on a farm," he lied.

"Did you have any brothers?"

"No. Just a sister."

"That's a shame. Rosemary might have got off her high horse and relaxed if there was another one of you to share."

"Well, I worked with my dad and we...we milked cows and stuff."

"Get to the good parts!"

Gabriel felt his skin tingling. "I'm sorry, what is it you want to know?"

"Was there a girl?"

"A girl?"

"Yes! Did you ever love a girl?"

He wasn't sure what the Princess wanted to hear, so he banked on a 'no' being the correct answer.

"But you must have! A boy such as yourself wouldn't have gone unnoticed."

"Well...there was one," he invented quickly. "But nothing came of it."

"What was her name?"

"Seren." It was the first name that came to mind.

"Did you...kiss?"

"No. Never. We just, talked. Every day. It was magical," he said, desperately conjuring the false romance. If he convinced her that talking was the most valuable part of a relationship, perhaps she'd keep her lips from him.

"Was she pretty?"

"Yes."

"I bet she was prettier than me."

"Oh...I doubt it..."

"But how would you know!" she cried suddenly. "You haven't even seen me yet!" Her husky voice was filled with fire. "I won't tolerate lies and false flattery. A man should be honest."

"I just meant -"

"Shh. You meant well, I'm sure. Here, give me your hand." She didn't wait for him to present it, she snatched his wrist in her pincer grip and raised his arm higher. "Touch my face. Go on. A blind man sees with his fingers."

Gabriel brushed his fingertips against a bulbous nose, a prominent forehead, thick eyebrows and thin lips. He could also detect traces of greasy residue.

"Beautiful."

Floriana had closed her eyes for the duration of his exploration and when she opened them again, she felt somewhat relaxed.

"Caleb, would you have done anything for Seren?"

"Yes," he said. "I probably would have."

"That's true love isn't it?"

"Yes, I suppose it is."

"Lay back," the Princess instructed.

His back and head met a mixture of pillows, which he sank between, feeling trapped. Floriana joined his side and placed an arm over his chest, like lovers might before falling asleep.

"Will you take a nap with me?"

Do I have a choice? he thought. "Okay."

"We can have a nap now and when the night comes, we can have a midnight feast! What do you think?"

"I think that sounds perfect," he replied, keeping the resentment from his voice.

"I think you're perfect," she said and nuzzled against his neck. "Sweet dreams, my future Prince."

Chapter 16

Gabriel didn't sleep a wink. Not only was it the afternoon, but there was a cursed Princess rubbing her humongous nose into the flesh of his neck rather annoyingly. He couldn't tell how much time had past, or if the sun had dipped below the horizon, because the scarf remained around his eyes.

When Floriana sluggishly stirred awake, he kept very still. *If she thinks I'm sleeping, she might leave me alone*, Gabriel thought.

"I think I dribbled in my sleep," she announced, moving her hand to hover over Gabriel's face. With her thumb and forefinger, she pinched his nostrils together, until he was forced to open his mouth and breathe.

"If you sleep any longer you won't be able to sleep tonight," she said, as if this justified her cruel 'awakening' technique. "Was it cosy for you?"

"Yes," he insisted. "Very."

"Good." She sat up and stretched. "Now, I'm going to inform the maids of my little feast tonight, to be held in this room. I'll have to invite my sister of course, to avoid suspicion. But don't worry, we'll have plenty opportunity to spend some time alone together."

"Brilliant," he said, feigning joy.

"It's going to be so much fun, I promise you."

"I can't wait."

"Well, I hope you don't mind, but precautions must be taken."

Gabriel had no idea what she meant, until he felt the Princess yank his left arm. To the bedpost, she tied his wrists with scarves.

"Sorry about how tight they are, but I wouldn't want you slipping over that balcony before we get better acquainted." She sighed. "I'm sure father will agree to a royal wedding if I wear him out with the idea."

Gabriel swallowed loudly.

Floriana flicked his nose. "See you in a bit."

He heard the door creak open and then shut with a snap until the only sound in the room was his own wild heartbeat.

*

Floriana tapped on Rosemary's door, shooing away the maid that lingered outside.

"What is it?" Rosemary asked idly, for she was in no mood for any sisterly conversation so soon after the last.

"A feast. Tonight. I must insist you come."

"Is the boy there?"

"Yes."

Rosemary's heart did a somersault. Another boy in the palace; such a rarity. It was so very wrong, but she wouldn't say no to some gossip if it were harmless enough.

"I'll come, if you promise you'll set him free

soon."

"I can't promise you that. But come meet him anyway."

Rosemary huffed loudly. "Fine. As long as you have the maids bake scones for the occasion."

"I was just on my way to the kitchens."

"What time shall I come?"

"Midnight."

Rosemary knew her sister would say midnight. It was when their father was most likely to be snoring away in his chambers and the maids would be in the underbelly of the palace, swapping stories and dreaming of marrying her brother, no doubt.

"I'll see you there."

Floriana left for the kitchens at a brisk pace, ignoring the maids that swished by with bundles of towels and bed sheets, or heated water in big metal buckets for the King's bath.

She knew her father's routine; a bath fit for royalty, then a slow walk around the garden at dusk - a time when his daughters were forbidden to leave their rooms in case they should come face to face. It was the only time.

"Evening, Princess," a maid greeted, rushing by with a tall-necked bottle labelled *bath salts*.

In the kitchen, Floriana found the head chef sleeping at a jaunty angle on a high stool, her back propped against the long wooden table. She had a rolling pin tucked under one chubby arm and a hair net tied about her greasy hair. On the table, there sat a black cat with big yellow eyes, swishing its tail this way and that.

It had a mouse in its mouth, which wriggled in the last throes of death.

Floriana cleared her throat. The head chef - Ms. Jones to her fellow cooks - jumped with a start, raising the rolling pin high above her head.

"Princess Floriana! I beg you, forgive me." She fell to the floor on her big round knees and lowered her head in respect. The cat leapt from the table and joined the cook's side, dropping what was left of the bloodied mouse on the flagstone floor.

"What is that thing doing in here again?" Floriana demanded, gestering to the feline.

"She catches the mice that get in-"

"And sits on the table where you prepare our food?" she thundered.

"Sorry, Princess. But I do disinfect all the surfaces before cooking, I swear on my daughter's life." Ms Jones was sweating under her hair net. She didn't favour the look in the Princesses' eyes. It was a known fact that Floriana was just as bloodthirsty as her father. "Please, spare my kitty," she added, clutching the cat to her thigh with her free hand.

Floriana wrinkled her nose in disgust. "Whatever. I've come here with a request."

Ms Jones clambered to her feet.

"My sister and I would like a midnight feast, to be held in my bed chambers. Understand?"

"Yes, Princess."

"You are to tell the maids to leave the food outside my door after three sharp knocks. They are not to linger when the food has arrived."

"Understood."

Floriana made her way to the stairs and then turned, "Oh, and Rosemary wants scones. Fresh ones. You know we can tell if they're not."

"Yes, Princess." Ms Jones nodded her head.

"Good. That's all."

The cook wiped her hands on her apron and reached up for the strings attached to big bronze bells. It appeared the maids were no longer in with a chance of an early night. The ringing vibrated through the palace.

*

Seren had persuaded Annabel to get some rest when the darkness had settled in for more than a few hours. She couldn't bear to see the girl pacing around the hut like a mad woman, raving about Gabriel being hurt and alone somewhere; maybe even dead. So, she'd made a pot of tea, mixing it with two teaspoons of lemon balm to help induce sleep. As soon as Annabel's head hit the blankets, she was out like a flame.

Seren sat on the doorstep for a while, thinking, wondering where on earth the boy could be. She doubted he'd deserted the girl because he'd shown her so much care and affection! Then what else?

She chewed her fingernails to bits whilst watching the stars twinkling overhead. She listened to the trees as they talked in creaks and groans to one another. When her eyes couldn't bear to stay open any longer, she allowed her head to rest against the doorframe and her vision to flicker in and out of consciousness.

"Seren?" came a whisper.

She opened one eye when a small hand touched her shoulder.

"He's not coming back is he?"

Gently, she placed her own hand over the child's - the same child she thought had been deep in the land of nod.

"We'll ask for help in the morning. There's nothing that can be done now."

Annabel's head drooped. She swaggered sleepily to her blankets, feeling lonely on her own beside the fire. But in a moment of unexpected empathy, Seren nestled down on the blankets beside her, the long strands of her hair fanning out across the floor.

They said nothing to each other, just slept.

*

When Rosemary gripped the handle of her sister's bedroom door, she could hear the voices within growing deadly silent. If it had been anyone else visiting her sister so late, suspicion would have been aroused. With the alibi of a midnight feast, given to the maids and Ms Jones, Floriana had covered her tracks well.

"There's food out here," she whispered, squeezing through the gap in the door. On the bear-hide with his legs crossed sat the fabled boy of Floriana's ravings. He was rigid, both hands gripping his knees and his head slightly downcast. He did not turn when Rosemary approached, for he couldn't see her beneath the scarf.

Floriana was on her feet and in the corridor before her sister could cry 'fresh cream' and with a murmur of satisfaction, she pushed a silver trolley of goodies into her bedchamber.

"Ms Jones went above and beyond tonight. I guess I'll let her off about having that mangy cat on the table." She poked her finger in the top of the whipped cream balanced on a scone and sampled its sweet flavour. She then proceeded to pinch at the flakes of duck meat covered in a spectacular sauce, pushing it into her mouth and dropping bits all over the carpet.

"I've been holding off eating all afternoon for this. Though it wasn't hard, what with Caleb being here to talk to."

"So that's his name then? Caleb?"

Floriana nodded as she thumped down next to her sister on the pink floral settee. She held a pancake soaked in syrup under Rosemary's nose, which she coyly accepted.

"Here, hold out your hand," Floriana instructed, in an unkind tone.

Gabriel was unaware of whom she was speaking to, until she slapped a soggy pancake down against his palm.

"Eat. It's good," she said through a mouthful.

Gabriel nibbled at the syrupy treat with a nauseous stomach. He hadn't felt like eating from the moment he'd been manhandled into the Princess's bedroom; forced to lie through his teeth about girlfriends he'd never truly had and life on a farm, which he knew virtually nothing about. Luckily, she hadn't mentioned removing his scarf. Yet.

"He's very pale," Rosemary observed. She relaxed with great difficulty in the presence of the imprisoned male.

"I know. Like milk. It's beautiful isn't it?"

"What profession is he in?"

"Farmer. Until he left home to travel."

"I guess he wound up in the wrong Kingdom," Rosemary laughed, half-heartedly. Floriana shot her a look of disapproval, before busying herself with a bowl of strawberries and cream.

"What exactly do you propose to do with him? You can't keep him locked up in your room forever."

"Why not?"

"Because it's cruel. Someone might be looking for him."

"And?" Floriana chomped through the red fruit, seeds sticking between her teeth.

"Do you have family, Caleb?" Rosemary queried.

"A sister," he spoke up, then wiped his mouth on the back of his hand. He liked this girl's voice. It was soft and feminine, like a mother talking words of comfort to a child. She didn't have a single hint of meanness or aggression in her tone, like her sister did.

"Are you expected elsewhere?"

"Pfft!" Floriana cried, waving her hand at Rosemary. "Leave them wait. They'll soon be ecstatic when they discover he's going to marry into royalty."

Rosemary frowned, but it disappeared as Gabriel said, "I have a girl waiting for me, yes."

"See. He's already taken," she rebuked.

"She's old news. He told me nothing came of their relationship."

"It's my sister. She's...with a friend and she's young. She's probably wondering where I am."

"I'll have a maid send word that you're safe," Floriana falsely promised. She picked at a scone and placed the remaining half in Gabriel's hand for him to finish.

He withered inside. There would be no winning his freedom back tonight, he realised. All hope was devoured along with the midnight feast and he soon found a new fear clutching at his chest as Floriana decided to play a game of 'guess the captive's eye colour.'

"It's got to be grey. Like, stone grey," she mused, lying on the bear-hide in front of him with her elbow propped up so that her palm could support her head.

"You're scaring him," Rosemary objected.

"Green then." Floriana ignored her, tracing a finger over the dips where Gabriel's eyes were situated beneath the scarf. "A nice rich green colour." She sat up properly. "There's only one way to find out -"

"DON'T!" Rosemary screamed, jumping from the settee and grabbing a hold of her sister's hand.

Floriana wrenched her hand free and glowered at Rosemary with a fiery hate. "Never tell me what I can and can't do. You're not my mother."

"What are you thinking? What good is the curse

at this hour? You'll never keep him hidden if he's scrabbling up the walls in want of you!"

Rosemary could see her sister mulling this over.

"Don't you want love to be *real* one day? Not a stupid spell?"

"Let's be blatantly honest here, Sis'. I wasn't the one that mother gave the beauty gene to. If it isn't coated in magic, it will probably never be true love."

Rosemary had never realised her hard-hearted sister felt this way. There was a look of sadness in Floriana's eyes and Rosemary had to bite her own tongue to contain her retort. *It could be real for you, if you stopped being so wicked*, she thought. But instead said, "You'll find true love. But tonight, leave the boy be."

"Fine," she sighed, and rested a hand on Gabriel's thigh. "It can wait a while longer."

Content with her sister's decision to hold back, Rosemary decided it was time for bed. Lowering her lips to Floriana's crown, she kissed her affectionately on the top of her head and bid her goodnight. "And goodnight to you too, Master Caleb," she said, as she closed the door quietly behind her.

Chapter 17

"Here, take this and we'll roll it up about your waist," Seren said, proffering a skirt at Annabel. "You've worn that dress for far too long now. You can't go like that."

She said nothing as she slipped her dress hurriedly over her narrow shoulders and shimmied into the grey skirt with Seren's help. Seren then presented her with an off-pink blouse that was three times her size.

"I look silly," Annabel complained, poking at a puffy sleeve.

"This too," Seren added, and tossed the girl a light green cardigan that had a burn mark on one of the sleeves. "It's all I've got that isn't overly big."

"Thanks, I guess."

When the girls were dressed and fed at the rising of the green sun, they set off with a swift stride in the direction of the palace. Seren was adamant that asking around the village about a boy with midnight hair and two working hands wouldn't get them anywhere. People liked to keep to themselves and no one opened their mouthes if they thought it might get them in trouble. There was only one thing for it; a trip to the root of all problems.

"It's so big," Annabel mumbled as they advanced

on the palace walls. Instead of walking the lane on the outskirts, they had walked as the crow flies, cutting a straight path through homes and the market, where many of the King's people were already wandering around tables in search of goods.

"Rumour has it the King was never born into royalty – that he stole the throne from another and claimed it for his own. But no one who has lived long enough to confirm the rumour will utter a word against him."

"So he's not really a King at all?" Annabel pressed.

Seren shrugged and marched on, waving for the child to keep up and stay close. The crowds were increasing in magnitude and the sales pitches began to ring out from the market-folk.

Annabel was relieved when the market was behind them. She hated being pushed about and having her feet trod on. Her shoes weren't the best. She'd had them – granted they had been a ghostly mirage until recently – for hundreds of years. She doubted they'd last much longer. And she didn't expect her bare footed friend to have any spare ones in her tiny size.

The chill in the air bit at their ears as they weaved through a park, coated in falling leaves of red and gold. The trees seemed unhappy today, swatting at Seren as she passed.

"Cut it out!" she shouted, when a branch struck the back of her head.

Annabel was surprised when the trees ceased their games, but she remained vigilant in case a rogue branch chose to lash out at any moment.

When the park's plantation thinned, leaving a clear path ahead, the palace gates loomed high above them. Gold, like the sun Annabel remembered back home, they were four times as high as Seren and fifty times as wide.

"They're closed." Annabel heaved a sigh.

Seren wrapped her fingers around the golden bars and peered through the gap. Two knights stood a distance away, with their hands secured around the hilts of swords. They were guarding the main entrance into the palace; two ivory doors with lion's heads for door knockers.

"Hey!" Seren yelled. "Hey, come here. We need to speak with someone."

The knights slowly glanced at one another in amusement.

"Hey, I'm talking to you. This is an emergency. This child has lost her brother!" She rattled the gates, but it did not coax the knights any nearer.

"Miriam Matthews…is that you under that helmet?" she bellowed.

Wheezy barks from four legged birds split the morning air wide open and Annabel screeched in fear as they swooped so close, she could feel a claw against her scalp. They dispersed rapidly into the restless trees, sending leaves tumbling down to the grassy earth.

"Miriam Matthews, you owe me one and you know it!" Seren persevered. "Would you like me to tell the Priest your secret?"

One of the knights stood down from her post and

clattered over. She lifted the visor on her helmet as she drew nearer and stared fearfully at Seren through the bars that separated them.

"I helped you when you came to me," Seren pleaded. "If the Priest knew you bore his child, and that you wished it gone through any means necessary, he would curse you Miriam and you know it."

"I know, I know," she whispered sharply. "I never meant for it to go that far."

"I asked for nothing from you when I went in search of those herbs. Did I not?"

"No."

"And I told no one when you drank the mixture I'd brewed a whole three days and nights."

"What is it you want from me?" Miriam asked dejectedly.

"A presence with the King. It's important. Someone close to us is missing."

"The King does not grant audience to anyone these days unless it is his royal consort, royal advisor or his children."

"The Prince then. He has a good heart. He'll listen."

Miriam stared over her shoulder at the other knight who was craning her neck to get a look at the gathering by the gates. "What do you think the Prince can do for you, Seren? He has problems of his own that haunt him."

"He can grant me access to the dungeons," she said, matter of factly.

Miriam thought about it. "You promise never to

call a favour of me again?"

"Cross my heart and hope to die."

The knight nodded and from a chain beneath her armoured vest, she revealed a key; promptly unlocking the gate. "Stay close to me. And say nothing in the palace until I've spoken to the Prince myself."

Seren looked at Annabel to silently reiterate the importance of this.

"The King has been known to chop off the hands of women in the past too, so don't give him reason to today."

The knight at the door – Miriam's partner – looked suspiciously at the two girls as they entered the palace. Inside, Annabel gasped. The main entrance was fifty times bigger than Seren's hut. No, one hundred times bigger! It was made of shiny white marble, flecked with gold. And along the corridors leading off to the left, right, and directly in front (between two curved staircases) hung oil paintings.

"This way," Miriam called, taking the corridor to their right.

Annabel had to skip to keep up. She gaped at the bronze candle brackets shaped like mermaids and marvelled at the views of the courtyard and gardens from each passing window. They took a flight of stairs up to the second level and hurried along, passing a maid pushing a trolley with a half-eaten slice of toast on a plate, a pot of jam and a half jug of warmed milk.

"He's up at least," Miriam indicated the breakfast. "He loves jam."

Outside Prince Delwyn's bedchamber door,

Miriam straightened her back until it was as stiff as an arrow and then rapped hard on his door. It wasn't long before there came an answering voice.

"Who is it?"

"Miriam, my Prince."

"Is it important?"

The knight looked to Seren, who was nodding enthusiastically.

"Apparently, *yes*."

The door opened a crack and a single enchanting blue iris met the knight's. It scanned the corridor and the other two females in his presence. Feeling bolder, he opened the door all the way.

"What's going on?"

The Prince was dressed in baggy trousers and nothing more, shamelessly revealing his chest. He had not long woken from a fitful sleep and had yet to call for warm water so he could wash.

"I'm sorry to disturb you so early in the morning, but my friend here begged to see you. I would not have come if I didn't think it were of importance."

"I know, of course." Delwyn glanced over at Seren, who was staring fixedly back at him. "Have we met?"

"Briefly. At the market a few times."

"I see. Well, you'll have to wait until I'm clothed. I can't talk in this state. Wait for me in the throne room. My father won't be up for a while yet."

Miriam bowed and closed the door, just as the Prince reached for a white shirt hanging on the back of a chair.

Seren and Annabel waited in the King's throne room for near an hour, pacing around and leaning against various pillars. When Annabel hazarded a stroke of the gold throne with her fingertips, a knight at its side made a loud coughing sound in the back of her throat and shook her head in warning.

Seren reached for Annabel and pulled her close, petting her on the top of the head. They were anxious beyond description, wondering if somewhere in the palace, Gabriel still breathed.

The doors opened with such force that Seren jumped in fright, creating a chain reaction in the child who yelped at the noise of wood slamming into the walls. Prince Delwyn was in no mood for village pests and he was in no mood for delay, but his good and kind nature kept him from dismissing the two girls from his father's palace.

"My Prince." Seren curtsied.

Annabel did the same a second after her.

"What can I help you with?" he asked.

"We've lost someone very dear to us; fear that he's been cursed. Please, to settle the poor child's suspicions, may we visit the dungeons?"

"You think he's been cursed?" the Prince repeated.

"That, or dead."

Annabel shot a look of dismay at Seren. For all the words of comfort she whispered on the journey to the palace, she hadn't expected Seren to be so blunt about Gabriel's disappearance. It made fear squirm in her belly like poison and she started to cry.

"Please, help us. I don't know what I'll do without him," she sobbed.

Prince Delwyn's expression melted in pity.

"Only my sister, Floriana has left the ground recently. If anyone was cursed, she would have mentioned it –"

"But if you could check just the same," Seren pleaded.

The Prince bit the inside of his lip thoughtfully. He looked at the gentle beauty of the young woman before him, the slope of her eyebrows and the sharp slice of her cheekbones. He noticed the smear of mud on her neck that had gone amiss in her morning wash and the way her hair tumbled in natural waves. Also, he sensed power in this girl. She was strong willed. If she wasn't, she'd never have had the audacity to demand an audience with him in his own bedchamber!

"The dungeons are no place for a child. She can stay here."

"No!" Annabel wailed. "I want to go with you! I need to see him!"

Seren's spirits sank for the child, but she was determined to find Gabriel, to see that Annabel got her guardian and friend back. As much as she enjoyed the company, she didn't want to be lumbered with raising the girl by herself. It wasn't in her nature to mother other people's children.

She squatted down in front of Annabel and wiped her tears with the side of her hand. "I'll be back soon. I promise."

"I never realised how much I'd miss him once

he'd gone," she mumbled between hiccups.

"We'll get him back."

"Come now." Prince Dewlyn started for the exit, his hands clasped behind his back. His boots clunked against the floor and his sword rattled in its sheath. Seren studied his back - the way his shoulder bones protruded slightly through the tight fabric of his shirt. She almost tripped when a maid bustled by with a horde of tiny dogs, all tugging on leather leads.

"My sister's pets," the Prince threw over his shoulder in explanation. "They can be a handful."

Seren said nothing as her bare feet avoided a disconcerting wet patch on the floor.

"May I ask, how this missing boy is related to you?"

"He's not."

"Then why are you here?"

"I have little else to do," she admitted.

"Ever thought about joining my father's staff? Become a maid?"

She burst out laughing before she could hold her own tongue. "What, and walk doggies all day? Cleaning up poo?"

Prince Delwyn had not expected such brutal honesty and sarcasm from the stranger. "I suppose you're right. Here." He gestured for her to walk down a dirty set of stairs, made of worn stone. A chill came from below, making the strands of her hair dance around her face.

"Aren't you coming?"

"I won't go all the way in. They get rowdy when they see me."

She nodded and started the descent. When Delwyn pulled a set of keys from his pockets, the jangling of metal alarmed her. Raising a hand to her chest in surprise, she smiled nervously as he reached through the dim light to an iron gate.

"There are only one set of keys to this dungeon," he explained. "I had to claim them from my father's guard. Told them I had to speak with someone down here about the witch that cursed my sisters. My father would be seriously displeased if he knew you were here."

Seren went a fiery red colour. "I'm honoured that you're doing this for me."

He pushed the gate open and gently pressed a hand against her back. "Go on. Be quick."

Seren's bare feet squidged into the grime on the floor, making bile rise in her throat. It was too dark to make out what the floor was covered in precisely, but she didn't let it play on her mind for long. Rushing forwards down the narrow corridor, she peered hopefully through the bars of every cell, calling Gabriel's name.

There were men of all shapes and sizes, wallowing in filth. Their heads rested against the pitted walls, or in the muck on the cold floor and the sounds of groaning followed her at every corner.

"Gabriel? Cry out if you're here!" she shouted, her voice echoing back at her.

"I'm here!" came a cry.

Seren's heart fluttered and she bounded forwards, clawing at the bars of a cell. "Gabriel?"

A young boy chuckled hoarsely. He was naked and covered head to foot in mud. But he wasn't the boy she was looking for.

The stirring prisoners began to wail the names of the Princesses as Seren roused them from sleep unintentionally with her presence. Those that were under the curse begged for freedom so that they could return 'to their loved one.' Others, the genuine thieves and vandals of the Kingdom, watched with bitter expressions, spitting at Seren's feet as she went by.

When she'd come full circle, she came to the conclusion that Gabriel wasn't at the palace. And she wasn't sure if that was a good thing or a bad.

She shook her head at the Prince as he watched her approach.

"I'm sorry," he said.

"Not as sorry as he'll be when I get my hands on him," she replied, though her heart wasn't really in the threat.

Back in the throne room, Annabel lunged at Seren the moment she entered.

"Did you find him? Is he well? Is he cursed?"

"No child. He's not here."

Annabel stared vacantly between the bare footed woman and the handsome Prince that flanked her. In that moment, she felt her entire world crumble.

Chapter 18

Gabriel was beginning to wish that the Princess had taken the scarf from his eyes, just so they could get the inevitable over and done with. He was sick to his stomach of waiting around the sweet smelling room, with his hands tied to bedposts or his posture rigid in a bed beside her.

The pancakes and syrup, scones and cream gurgled in his belly after Rosemary's departure and he'd suffered a sleepless night, with the pincer like grip (even when she was dreaming) of Floriana

He wasn't sure how much more of this he could take before he yelled at the top of his lungs for help. He didn't care if he was tortured or cursed, cut and maimed; he wanted out.

"I'm just going to bathe. I'll bring you back something to eat if you're good," Floriana promised, as she slipped a velvet robe about her waist and dragged her bushy brown hair up from under the collar. "Won't be long, so sit tight." The door to her bedchambers closed with a *thunk*.

Gabriel tested the tightness of his bonds and growled low in his throat. The Princess was clearly a dab hand at tying knots and he cursed her silently, hating all there was to hate about her.

His mind wandered. He couldn't help thinking about poor Annabel. He prayed that Seren was looking after her. If the child died a second death because of him, he'd be in turmoil for all eternity – he just knew he would.

That was it. He'd decided there and then, whilst picturing the child's bright eyes that he would scream blue murder until a guard came running. Gathering up a lungful of air, he opened his mouth – and choked as the door opened with an audible *creak*.

There came the shuffling of a gown, to his ears best divination and a touch of soft skin upon his warm cheek.

"Are you okay, boy?"

"Rosemary?"

"Princess Rosemary," she corrected, but she did not sound afflicted by his disrespect.

He sat in silence, unsure of himself. Was she here to visit her sister, or him?

"She's bathing, yes?"

"Hmm," he said. He felt the familiar swell and pull of the Princess's curse working through him. Even without eye contact, it made him feel dreamy and somewhat in need of her. Funny though, it felt stronger in Rosemary's presence than in Floriana's.

"You have done nothing wrong, boy," she said, "but if my father finds you here, he won't think so."

"I want to leave. I want to return to my friends," he begged.

"Yes, I know."

"Can't you...help me?" he tried.

"And risk the wrath of my baby sister?"

His chest deflated, but he felt the comforting touch of her hand moving to his knee.

"You are a sweet boy. I can tell without looking into your eyes."

She wouldn't have said that if I were still a vampire, he thought.

"I want to help you," she continued. "But I can't think of any way I can do so without angering Flo'."

"I understand."

"Though, I think if our brother were to have a say in this, she might listen to him."

"Your brother? Prince Delwyn?"

Rosemary bit her lip and glanced over her shoulder.

"The maid's change the bed sheets in two days' time. She'll want you properly hidden away, or cursed by then, Caleb."

Gabriel sighed. "My name isn't Caleb. It's Gabriel. I lied to your sister." He lowered his head. "Forgive me."

Rosemary removed her hand. "Gabriel is a much nicer name."

"I was scared," he admitted. "I don't get scared often, and yet -"

"Shh," she soothed. "I know."

He sunk his head into her awaiting palm and rested his chin there.

"I'll get you out," she vowed.

He nodded against her skin. He wanted to believe

her, but all hope was fluttering out of the open window to the balcony, and into the green tinted sky.

*

Rosemary passed her sister in the corridor on the way to her chambers. She received a dirty and suspicious look from her, but Rosemary smiled warmly and continued on her way as if nothing suspicious of the sort had happened.

Floriana's hair was damp and wavy and her skin was flushed with the heat of a good scrub. "Rose," she called, before her sister disappeared from sight.

"Yes?" Rosemary stopped abruptly with a tingling up her spine.

"Lunch in the garden today?"

"We have the weather for it," she agreed.

Floriana turned and left, and Rosemary hurried on.

Rosemary bided her time in the adjoining room to her bed chambers; her very own art department as she liked to think of it. Her father had sent maids far and wide to gather paints and dyes, canvases and charcoals, chalks and pencils, so she could work away the hours immersed in her own imagination, pouring life and colour onto blank surfaces. Watercolours were her favourite. She worked this clear, warm day on a pale face, the colour of coy carp scales. She then painted furrowed eyebrows in ebony shades and proceeded to swish a smaller brush into the shapes of eyes. She painted them blue; her guess at Gabriel's colouring.

When she was finished she stared at her work, lost

in the image of a boy she hardly knew. She touched his cheek with a fingertip and thought about the heat from his skin burning beneath it –

A knock came.

It startled her, sending the dirty paint water with the used brushes in all over her paper. The murky liquid swallowed Gabriel's likeness on the page, bringing the black of his midnight hair into a thick puddle that morphed his features.

"Rose?"

"One moment!" she yelled.

She quickly snatched up the ruined painting and folded it four times, discarding of it in a pile of rubbish waiting to be collected by the cleaner.

Impatient by nature, Floriana pushed her way into the art room and stopped in the doorway. She was dressed in a vermillion gown with billowing sleeves and an extended train that slid along the floor behind her. Her hair had been plaited neatly down her back. She looked womanly and presentable for a change.

"What are you doing in here?" Floriana walked to the table and picked up a blank page, which was damp from the water that had soaked the sheet above it. "What's this? Abstract art?" She turned it this way and that. "Not your best work."

Rosemary blushed. "Why are you here? Is something the matter?"

"Um...lunch?" Floriana replied sardonically. "I've been sat in the garden waiting for you a whole half hour. I almost gave your sandwiches to the dogs."

"I'm so sorry! I was so busy, I let time get away

from me."

"Hmm," Floriana mumbled. "Come on then. While the sun is out. I've asked Martha to bring our bows from the armoury. It's clear enough for a spot of target practise. First to ten bulls eyes?"

"But you always win," Rosemary remarked, trying to keep her sister happy in any way she could. A bit of flattery went a long way with her sibling.

"Well, I'll try and do it blindfolded if it makes you feel any better," Floriana grinned.

They left the art room, walked through Rosemary's neat and tidy bedchamber and made their way to the gardens with buoyant spirits. All the maids greeted them on passing and outside, their dogs frolicked in the grass, rolling onto their backs in glee as their owners reclined on chairs.

"Do you suppose she's really up there?" Rosemary wondered, picking up a frosted glass of lemon water.

"Who?" Floriana replied, crossing her big feet at her ankles and bringing a fan to her face, gently wafting cool air over her oily skin.

"The witch. Do you think she's in the mountains? I mean, what evidence do we have?"

"I'm sure Delwyn's knights will find her, by killing one old hag at a time."

"But the wrong ones are dying. Don't you think that's wicked?"

"One less witch in the world is better for everyone, Rose."

Rosemary sipped her lemon water sedately,

watching her sister tickle Marmeduke's belly. He was a spaniel, with big floppy ears and a brown wet nose; their favourite pet. Marmeduke was the first animal their mother, the Queen – rest her soul – had ever given them.

"Is the boy safe?"

Floriana scowled. "As safe as can be. Why? Jealous?"

"Not at all."

"He's very handsome."

"I suppose."

"You know he is."

"It's hard to tell with that scarf masking half his face."

"Well, I saw most of his face at the market. And he's a fine looking lad. The finest I've ever seen in the Kingdom."

Rosemary agreed, but did not voice her opinion. "Keep him fed," she suggested.

"Obviously."

They stared at the grounds, illuminated with spears of sunlight through fluffy white clouds. The flowers bobbed and squealed as the dogs dug holes amongst them and the maids in the distance dragged out a target for archery practise.

Floriana's maid, Martha, joined them. "Your equipment, Princess." She held their bows forth and two quivers full of arrows.

"Prepare to lose, Sister," Floriana enthused, jumping from her seat.

Rosemary smiled and took her bow. "You first, sister."

*

When the archery practise drew to an end hours later, and Floriana had beaten Rosemary eleven bulls eye's to three, she practised a loud and satisfying yawn.

"I'm feeling awfully tired."

"Really?" Floriana let an arrow loose and hit the target, shattering an arrow already at its centre. She hissed in triumph and lowered her bow.

"It must have been that midnight feast," Rosemary lied. "I think I'll lay down for an hour."

"I'm heading into the market. See If I can't find some new shirts for Caleb. I can't ask the maids or they'll be suspicious."

Rosemary nodded in understanding and signalled for Martha. The maid had been standing in the shade of a pear tree, watching the Princesses compete. Without a word, she took Rosemary's things and stood in wait for instruction from Floriana, who didn't look as if she wanted to stop practising anytime soon.

"One more round, Martha. I want to see if I can get ten in a row."

"Yes, Princess."

"Here, why don't you try?"

Rosemary slid away, leaving the maid to struggle with a bow and to endure the fiery competitiveness of her sister as she loosed arrows at the target with battle cries that would startle a mole in its bed.

She kept her stride slow and elegant, until she reached the gate with the ugly stone gargoyles leering over the wall – her least favourite fixtures at the palace grounds. On the other side of the wall, out of Floriana's hawk-like sight, she hurried into the palace, picking up her skirts as she went. Her sandals slapped at the marble as she tore down the east wing corridor – past the glorious portraits of her mother and father through the years of their marriage.

When she bumped into Emily, she demanded a scarf from her pinny, which the maid gave her without questioning. And at her brother's door, she tied the scarf around her head, nodding curtly at his knight, Elanor, who was standing guard.

She knocked on Delwyn's door and waited blindly for an answer.

"What now?" came a voice from within.

The door swung open with a whoosh of air that disturbed Rosemary's gown.

Delwyn let out a gasp. He had not expected to see her here before him, unannounced.

"Rose!"

"May I speak with you? It's urgent."

Delwyn scratched the back of his neck nervously. He didn't like to see his sister's eyes bound in such a manner, but it was very rare she paid him a visit.

"Certainly, come in." He took her hand and guided her carefully into his room. She tripped over the rug, but didn't complain and when she was seated, he let go of her.

"To what do I owe this pleasure?" he asked calmly, folding his arms over his chest. He'd been exercising before she'd disturbed him, doing sit-ups and push-ups and all the other kinds of 'ups' that kept him fit enough for combat – should he need to go into battle.

Rosemary turned her hands over and over in her lap. "There's a bit of a problem."

"Okay."

"Floriana is holding a boy hostage in her room."

"She's what?!" he exclaimed.

"She knows it's forbidden and I've tried telling her, but she won't listen to me."

The Prince raged with anger. "You'd think she'd have the decency to leave well alone after the last one!"

Rosemary could hear her brother pacing as she thought back to Floriana's previous prisoner. Their father had made a spectacle out of it, to both scold Floriana and his people for allowing such a thing to happen. The poor boy had been hung by the neck in the courtyard and Rosemary had been sick for days at the sight of it; making herself bed-bound as she replayed the swinging body in her mind over and over.

She swallowed down the pain of remembering the tragedy.

"He'll do it again, if he finds out," she said. "We need to get the boy out of here."

There came a click of fingers. "Well, I'll be damned." Delwyn paused. "The girls that came here this morning were looking for a lost friend."

Rosemary stopped moving her hands. "Then it must be Gabriel."

He sighed loudly. "When is our sister going to learn?"

"I fear she never will. There's something terrible

inside her, Delwyn. I know she's our blood, but she takes after father in so many ways. I...I hate being near her."

Her brother stood in silent understanding. He sank to his knees and gripped his sister's hands in his own. "Distract her tonight. I'll go to her chambers and get him out safely. But make sure you're both out of sight." He thought about being cursed and shuddered. He'd come close too many times before now, but had thankfully never fallen under the witches spell.

"Where should I take her?"

"Think of something. Anything. I'll get the boy out of the palace."

"I'm sorry to have to put this on you. He's genuinely a sweet lad and absolutely terrified. He doesn't deserve this."

Delwyn rose to his feet and his sister rose with him.

"Be gone by midnight."

"We will."

He led her to the door. "And Rose."

"Yes?"

"Sorry we had the wrong witch yesterday."

She smiled sweetly. "Brother, you have nothing to be sorry about."

He nodded, though her words failed to settle his stomach.

"Good luck," she whispered.

"And to you," he replied.

Chapter 19

Seren had to drag Annabel from the palace kicking and screaming.

"Stop making a spectacle of yourself! Do you want the King to chop your hands off?" she scolded, tugging the girl through the open gates and giving Miriam a thankful nod on passing.

"He can't have left me! He must be in there!" she wailed and whimpered, yanking on Seren's arm to stop her from ploughing on. But she wasn't strong enough to stop her and soon gave up trying.

Seren listened to the child's sobbing the whole way to the hut and when they were safely inside, made pancakes to give the child something to stifle all the noise.

Maybe what I feared would happen, has happened after all, Seren thought. *The boy has dumped the child on me. And yet he seemed so honest and caring with her.*

Annabel quietened when her belly was full and sat on the front step of the hut, staring at the waving trees on the outskirts of the woods and the grasshoppers bouncing off the rocks at her feet.

Seren stirred a herbal tea in a pot over the wood burner, filled two mugs and drew up beside Annabel. She handed her a mug, which she took and scooted up next to her on the step.

"Perhaps it's time to tell me your story," Seren said. "Why you and Gabriel are really here?" she prompted.

Annabel sniffed and wiped her nose on the back of her hand.

"He told me not to," she muttered sheepishly. "But if he's truly gone, I guess there's no use keeping it a secret anymore."

Seren blew cool air into her mug, dispersing the steam. She waited for the child to speak.

"Gabriel and me... we weren't always like this. I mean, we *were*, a very long time ago. But it's only recently that we turned back."

"I don't think I follow you."

Annabel sighed. "I was dead. And so was he."

Seren blinked a few times in quick succession. "Excuse me?"

"He killed me. Drank my blood. And I haunted him."

"But...But you're flesh and bone."

"I am *now*. We came through a mirror into this world and it changed us. Made us whole again."

"So let me get this straight. You were ghosts?"

"Well, I was. He was a vampire."

Seren looked astonished. "A *vampire*?"

"Yes. You know, one of those blood-sucking creatures that never die? He met his maker a few days ago... the first vampire. She made us come here."

Mug of tea completely neglected now, Seren stared fixedly at Annabel. She couldn't believe what she was hearing.

"She said we had to bring her back someone to love. Someone she could marry, or else she'd kill us. For good this time," Annabel continued, and a little sob burst from her mouth. "I guess...she got fed up...of waiting." Tears flowed freely again.

"You said you came through a mirror and it changed you?"

Annabel could only manage a nod.

"That sounds like powerful witchcraft to me."

"Probably. But who cares? She got to Gabriel!"

"We don't know that for sure," Seren said comfortingly.

"Where else could he be?"

Seren felt a weight building on her shoulders. If Annabel was marked for death, the 'maker' she spoke of may already be on her way to the hut.

She shuddered and rushed back inside, pulling jars of herbs from the shelves, as well as a bottle of salt from a cupboard.

"What are you doing?" Annabel watched in puzzlement as the young woman swooped around the kitchen, throwing bits and bobs into a glass bowl and mashing them up with a wooden utensil.

"I know enough magic of my own to cast a little protection spell over the hut. But it'll only work when we're inside. If we leave, we're on our own."

Annabel took little steps towards Seren and then

timidly looped her hands around her thin waist. Seren froze, unsure of herself and then patted the girl lightly on the head. She then smiled weakly. "We all need a friend in dark times. Trust me, I know."

*

Rosemary sucked in a breath before rapping loudly on Floriana's door. She had waited a sufficient amount of time in her room, pacing and fretting, painting and pondering until a maid by the name of Alesha had alerted her to her sister's return from the market.

"Who is it?" came a gruff bark from within.

"It's me, Flo'. Let me in, quick. I have something to tell you!"

Floriana begrudgingly opened the door to her sister, turning her back on her almost immediately to pursue her four-poster bed. Gabriel was sitting there with his legs dangling over the edge of the mattress. Beside him rested a plate of spaghetti and mincemeat.

"We were in the middle of dinner." Floriana picked up a fork and twisted it around the plate with a screech of metal against porcelain. She shoved the ample amount of food into her guest's partially opened mouth and watched him chew it in fascination. "I *have* been feeding and watering him, in case you were wondering."

"He's not a dog. He's a human being."

"I know that!" she spat. "Anyway. What did you want to tell me?"

Rosemary bounced down onto the mattress on Gabriel's other side and assumed an expression of pure elation. "I have just received the most amazing news!"

Floriana lowered the fork. It was very rare she saw her sister this excited about anything and curiosity welled inside her instantly. "What?"

"A unicorn, Flo'. In the west woods."

Floriana's eyes widened.

Rosemary was well aware that her bloodthirsty sister had dreamed of taking down one of the mythical and legendary creatures of their father's fairy tales, spoken to them at night when they couldn't sleep. She also knew it was Floriana's ambition to snare and tame one, or at the least, kill one for its horn.

"Are you fooling with me?"

"Not at all!"

"Who told you?"

"Alesha came to my chambers to tell me! It seems one of the knights spotted it when they were out hunting rabbits this afternoon. It slipped away, but they're sure it's still near. Can you imagine? A unicorn in our very own woods!" Rosemary appeared so excitable; she almost believed her own lie.

"We *must* catch it for ourselves."

"Yes. And we will. Tonight at eleven, we'll sneak out."

"But can't we go now?"

"Wouldn't you rather go with me? If we go now, father will make the guard join us. I want it to be our own adventure. Just me and you, like we always used to dream about."

"Hmm. Imagine everyone's faces when they see us riding home on the unicorn's back."

"So you'll join me tonight?"

Floriana grinned uncontrollably, "A ravenous wolfman couldn't keep me away."

Rosemary placed a hand over her sister's shoulder and stood up. "I'm so excited."

"Me too."

Gabriel received another mouthful of food. The spaghetti was chewy like rubber. It had been over-cooked and had lingered on the plate far too long. But he was grateful none the less. He'd been forced to sit in silence, tied to the post of Floriana's bed, for hours upon hours. It had almost been a relief when she'd returned with dinner.

"Might I join you?" he tried.

A burst of mocking laughter escaped Floriana's mouth. "Do you think I'm an imbecile? Of course you can't join us. But when we're married one day, we can go hunting together all the time if you'd like?"

"Sounds great," he groaned, slouching.

"I'll choose to ignore your sarcasm," Floriana quipped, forcing another mouthful of spaghetti so hard into his mouth, the fork almost chipped a tooth.

Rosemary flinched and decided to leave them both to it.

*

When evening came, Rosemary ate her own meal at the table on her balcony with only a caged songbird for company. She left most of her own spaghetti dinner untouched because her stomach was tied in knots. Her plan was rolling over and over in her head. It was simple:

take Floriana into the woods for a fruitless hunting expedition and on her return, Gabriel would have vanished with the help of her brother. What could go wrong?

"I'd better get ready," she said to the bird, which cocked its head to the side to listen.

She selected from her wardrobe a pair of red leather trousers, a white long-sleeved blouse with silver buttons and a black cloak with a hood, in case it should rain. Sending Alesha to the armoury, she waited for her bow and in the meantime, strapped a dagger to her belt should she need it.

Fear of a wolfman crept up her spine, even though Delwyn was adamant he'd slaughtered the only one ever seen or heard of in the Kingdom. There'd been no reports of another since, but to be on the safe side, she armed herself with a pistol containing silver bullets that she'd kept hidden in a dusty box under her bed.

Floriana was so eager for the hunt, she came to Rosemary's room first.

"How will we get outside without alerting the guards?"

"How's your upper body strength?"

"Adequate."

Rosemary winked and pulled from the bottom drawer of her wide mahogany chest, a tangle of sheets all joined together expertly with knots. With a thud of boots, she made her way to the balcony, which was illuminated with nothing but moonlight. She tied the end of the sheets to the ledge and let them tumble down.

"You've become rather daring. I like it," Floriana

mused, hitching up her own cloak and climbing over the edge.

It was quite a long distance down, but luckily for them, Rosemary's balcony overlooked the gardens, where only a single guard patrolled every two hours. They had plenty of time to climb down into a patch of violets before either of them was seen.

The night was cold but clear. The lawn was sprinkled with dew and the flowers all slept peacefully in their beds of earth. Rabbits scampered left right and centre, enjoying the freedom of the land, until Floriana's feet touched the ground. They scattered in terror in the direction of the hedges that encircled their mother's favourite patch; a maze of bushes, trees and benches with a fountain at its centre.

Rosemary struggled on her own decent, gripping the sheets in panic. Every time she moved to lower herself, her heart leapt into her mouth.

"Come on, Rose!" Floriana called.

Rosemary's bow peeked over her shoulder and scraped against the palace wall. Her thighs burned with the effort of gripping the assortment of knots at various intervals. But when she was more than half way, a sudden wash of fearlessness spread through her and she let go entirely.

Floriana jumped aside as her sister crashed to the earth.

Rosemary's feet hit the ground and buckled under her, sending her into a roll that scattered her arrows from the quiver at her back. She cursed and scrabbled for them, her sister joining her.

"Remind me to teach you how to perfect the art of escaping," Floriana whispered.

The sister's shared a smile and when the arrows had been returned to their rightful place, they ran off into the night, as if a wolfman were snapping at their heels.

Chapter 20

Prince Delwyn wiped sweat from his brow as he looked up at the old cuckoo clock on his wall. It had belonged to his grandmother before she died, and his bedchambers had happened to be hers once. He hadn't the heart to take the clock down, but in a fit of annoyance during his teenage years, he'd broken the cuckoo out.

When the clock struck midnight, he made his way to Floriana's room. The maid's and knight's still awake at this hour all wished him a 'good night' as he passed by, but asked nothing of his purpose for being up so late. It wasn't unnatural for him to visit the kitchens for a snack in the evenings, or a cold glass of water.

One of his knights, by the name of Esmelda, had been posted outside Floriana's room this particular evening, standing to attention when he approached.

"She's not there, my Prince."

Delwyn stopped, his hand on the doorknob.

"She visited her sister about an hour ago."

He fumbled for an excuse, the candlelight from the mermaid sconces dancing over his blushing cheeks. "I know, Ez.' That's why I came. Fancied doing a bit of schoolboy pranking, if you catch my drift. It's not often I have the chance to do something wicked to a sibling. And isn't it a brother's right?"

Esmelda scowled, shifting from one foot to another, but said nothing more. It wasn't her place to after all.

Delwyn opened the door a crack and squeezed inside, grinning mischievously at the knight as he closed it behind him.

Inside, he rested his back against the door and breathed deeply. He took a moment to allow his eyes to focus on the large room, alit with nothing but firelight. The corners were all dark and the shadows, off-putting.

"Hello?" he whispered, as quiet as was humanly possible.

He walked to the bed, but found nothing. He lowered himself to the floor and checked underneath, but found nothing also.

"Boy? I'm here to get you out –"

He stepped onto the balcony, but it was empty and scouted out the adjoining room full of Floriana's neglected, half-finished pieces from various hobbies – a wooden rocking horse, led on its side with no base; a sowing machine covered in a sheet at a table; flower pots on the window ledge with half dead, dried up tomato plants bent over double; a china doll with a broken, half painted face; a pair of pink ballet slippers dirty with mud; an old typewriter, also covered from a time when she'd informed her father she was going to be a great play write. But no boy.

He was beginning to think Rosemary had been mistaken, when there came a scratching sound from the bedchamber. It took him a moment to locate it, but as he opened the door of his sister's grand wardrobe, he found what he'd been looking for.

Gabriel was curled up amongst a sea of shoes, his eyes, hands and mouth bound with scarves so that only his poor nose could take in oxygen. He looked like an Egyptian mummy and had been scratching at the door with his fingernails, when the Prince's distant voice had woken him. He'd given no thought to what would come of him if he revealed his presence. All he cared about now was ending this imprisonment once and for all.

"You poor lad. Come here," the Prince said, untying the knots at the back of his head and then freeing the boy's hands.

When he could open his eyes, it took them a minute or two to adjust to the light. A stinging, searing pain filled his eye sockets and he looked up with a wince at his saviour like a new born baby.

Delwyn lifted Gabriel from the pile of shoes, knocking gowns from hangers with his head as he pulled him to his feet.

"Are you alright?"

"I'll live," Gabriel muttered. "Thank you for coming."

"Don't thank me. Thank Rosemary. She wanted to see to it you got out of here alive."

Gabriel nodded, his chest swelling with gratitude.

"But we have a problem. There's a knight outside the door. If she sees you leaving the room with me, she's under strict obligation to report it to my father."

Gabriel paled at this.

"I think I can get rid of her. Just stand in that room

out of sight for the time being until I return for you."

Gabriel slipped away with no further prompting, waiting amongst the discarded machinery and the odds and ends of Floriana's past failures. He almost expected to find a skeleton in there, of the previous boy she'd imprisoned – maybe pinned to the wall as a reminder of her own insanity. He shivered at the thought.

Delwyn rushed to the door and opened it a crack.

"Psst! Ez!" he hissed.

The knight turned her head and eyed the Prince in confusion.

"Do me a favour, would you? It'll only take a moment." He feigned giggling and cupped a hand over his mouth to stifle it. "Go to the kitchens and fetch me a pot of honey with a spoon. You can tell Ms Jones it was my doing, I promise."

Esmelda nodded her head and reluctantly left her post – there was no Princess around to guard at this hour so what harm would it do to make a detour to the kitchens? But before she left, she pulled a scarf from her pocket.

"Forgive my forwardness, Prince Delwyn. But would you keep this handy in case Floriana should return? I'd hate to be blamed for your lack of care." She said this with a hint of scorn. It didn't seem like the Prince to go about the palace without a blindfold handy, especially in his cursed sister's bedroom!

"Thanks Ez. Now, hurry before she catches me."

Esmelda marched down the corridor to the right and when she'd disappeared from sight, Delwyn bounded into the bedroom once more, throwing open the door to the adjoining room.

"Quickly. We haven't got much time. Put this on." He threw a cloak at the boy from a pile of clothing bought by Floriana at the market that same day. She'd kept her word and paid for some clean clothing for her prisoner, but had left it draped over a chair in her haste to leave with Rosemary for whatever reason his sister had concocted.

With the cloak on his back and his eyes slightly more adjusted to the dim lighting, he chased after the Prince, taking the corridor to the left.

"Keep close to my side," Delwyn warned him. "I know it's tempting, but don't run until it's safe to."

Their strides were long and swift. When a maid bustled by, Delwyn flashed her a flirtatious smile that made her blush instead of suspicious as to why a strange boy followed him.

On the ground floor, they weren't so lucky. A knight put a hand on Delwyn's shoulder and stopped him in his tracks as they reached the main entrance.

"Who's this?"

"A cousin."

"I wasn't told," the knight said. She was twice his age and worn in the face, less likely to be tricked.

"He arrived late this evening. I'm taking him on a tour of the grounds. We can't sleep."

"I've been here all evening and no one has come through that front door."

"Well, that's because he came through the back," the Prince replied, forcing some authority into his tone. "And I don't much like being questioned on the matter.

Can't a Prince and his cousin go for a walk without being harassed?"

The knight's eyes narrowed. "I suppose so."

"Good."

He marched on, opening the front door and scowling at the knight as they went.

The bite of cool night air almost made Gabriel weep. He froze, in awe of the stars and closed his eyes as a breeze nipped his ears. Freedom had never tasted so sweet to him.

"Now, we run," Delwyn whispered, grabbing Gabriel's arm and jostling him from his trance.

*

Rosemary could hardly keep up with her sister's movement through the west woods. Floriana was stealthy and fearless, like a hungry tiger prowling. It was both impressive and scary.

Whereas Rosemary liked to take up peaceful activities at the palace, her sister had become more of a predator as the years went by. When a deer happened to cross her line of vision, Floriana let an arrow fly, shooting it down where it stood. The deer bucked and whined before collapsing, letting out its final breath with fear ripe in its eyes.

"She's pregnant," Rosemary cried in despair. She bent down and touched the deer's swollen belly, where a strange movement confirmed it for her. Without hesitation, she took her knife and gently cut at the deer's stomach. Blood pooled around the open wound and splashed over her knees, which she'd pressed against the animals dwindling warmth.

Floriana gripped Rosemary roughly under her armpit and tried to yank her away. "What are you doing? We don't have time to play God."

"I'm not playing God! I'm correcting a mistake."

Floriana let go. "Just leave it, would you?"

"I'm the oldest. Stop telling me what I can and can't do."

"We came out here for a *reason.*"

Rosemary bit her lip to refrain from hissing the truth at her sister; that their hunt was nothing but a distraction, pointless and stupid.

She worked away at the poor creatures flesh. Making a deep enough and wide enough hole, she reached inside the mess of slimy heat and gripped onto what she hoped was the fawn. With a wheeze of strain, she tugged it free, until an alien mound of blood and wriggling landed on her lap.

"That's foul," Floriana grumbled, masking her nose with her free hand.

Rosemary pierced the sack and watched the fawn slosh out. It didn't move. She wiped its nose and mouth with the sleeve of her dress and rubbed its throat. Floriana watched, but made no attempt to help.

"Come on," Rosemary whispered to the animal. "Please. Wake up."

But the tiny fawn didn't move.

Rosemary dropped her knife in solemn defeat, choking back tears.

"Never mind, sis. Now let's get a move on."

Rosemary didn't get up, or try to push the fawn away. She remained crumpled on the floor, fixated on the death before her.

"Get up, Rose!"

"No."

"This was your idea!"

"I know it was."

Floriana reached down and wrenched the arrow from the deer's side, frustration building inside her at a rapid pace. "Why all the excitement and risk if you're not even bothered about finding this unicorn with me?" The hand holding the arrow lowered. "Unless..." Her voice trailed off.

Rosemary petted the fawn in a useless fashion. She knew she should get up and go, but she didn't have the energy to move. She was exhausted and wracked with guilt.

"There is no unicorn...is there?"

Rosemary wiped her eyes, leaving smears of animal blood on her face. "Yes there is," she muttered tiredly.

"No. There isn't."

"Yes there is!"

"You brought me out here on purpose."

"Don't be so silly."

"You don't even like hunting. I mean look at you, one dead deer and you're a weeping, pathetic mess."

"I like to hunt. Just not when it's unnecessary like this." She gestured at Floriana's double-murder as she rose from the ground.

"I see you better than you might think," Floriana

said crisply. She met her sister's eyes, moving closer in proximity. "He's gone hasn't he?"

Rosemary took a step back. "I have no idea what you're talking about."

"Caleb. He's gone."

She was silent.

"ANWSER ME!"

"I have no idea what you're talking about," Rosemary repeated, her voice wavering.

Floriana set off at a run, leaving Rosemary stunned and alone in the woods. She raced after her, sending sleeping birds into a frenzy as she yelled and pleaded for her to slow down.

"If he's gone, you're dead to me," Floriana yelled.

"Flo! Wait, come back!"

Floriana sprinted through the darkness, her eyes trained to see in very little light after many archery lessons in nothing but the glow of the moon. She avoided the darker shadows and followed the silver light reflected off the shrubs and grass. Her breathing became ragged, but she didn't stop, for she hated being made a fool of by anyone. Her anger fueled her, and her heart beat with the utmost disappointment in her sibling, who was tumbling blindly behind her.

At the gates of the palace, she didn't try to be secretive in her return. She bounded through, and came face to face with the unexpected...

Chapter 21

Prince Delwyn almost bit his tongue clean off when he'd reached the closed gates.

He had planned on giving Gabriel a leg up, so that the boy could climb over and be on his way, but in his final stride, a ghostly pale face loomed before him, equally as surprised.

"No!" he screamed, bringing his hands to his eyes.

But it was too late.

The magic worked through his eye sockets and into his blood, sending quivers and shivers of uncontrollable agony through his body, followed by a tingling of pleasure and dreamy enchantment.

"Delwyn!" Floriana exclaimed, gripping the bars of the gates in astonishment.

Her brother had stopped writhing and was walking mellowly towards her now, disregarding a stunned Gabriel, who had wisely closed his eyes the moment he'd noticed the silhouette's ahead.

Delwyn reached his hand through the gates and stroked Floriana's oily cheek in admiration. She flinched away from his touch.

"Sweet, sweet angel. I'm so glad I found you," he

said, unabashed by her blatant disgust.

"What's going on?" Gabriel called over. "Prince Delwyn?"

The Prince ignored the boy and stretched his fingers through the bars. He wanted desperately to reach Floriana. His heart, soul and mind begged him to hold her in his arms. He wanted her. He needed her. He'd stop at nothing to have her.

"Delwyn!" came a shriek, as Rosemary caught up with her sister, all bloody with deer guts. She clamped her eyes shut so as not to curse her brother, but in a moment of honed listening, she realised it didn't matter.

"Look what you've done!" Floriana bellowed, rounding on her sister.

"ME?" she yelled back.

"If you hadn't have interfered, this would never have happened!"

Rosemary lowered her eyes in shame. She was right.

"Rosemary? Are you there?" Gabriel asked. He was still standing blind, only vaguely aware of the Prince scrabbling at the bars in front of him.

"Yes she's here. My perfect big sister. Full of light and goodness. Trying to protect a street rat and as a result, she's cursed our brother."

"I didn't."

"And she got a deer and her baby killed."

"No!" Rosemary whimpered. "No, I didn't mean-"

Floriana grabbed her sister's shoulders and shook her. "You did this to us! You evil witch!"

Rosemary cried tears of sorrow and Gabriel felt his heart jolt for the girl. He wanted to look into her face and tell her it would be okay – that she'd tried her best – but he knew he was safer on his side of the fence.

"Please, let me stroke your hair. Let me brush your lips with mine!" Delwyn demanded. He was becoming frustrated and started inching up the gate.

"Get down you idiot!" Floriana snapped. "Before someone hears us."

"It's too late now. They'll all know when they see him," Rosemary admonished quietly. She was gripping her arms where her sister had dug fingernails into her flesh.

Delwyn was half way up now.

"Stop it!" Floriana whacked his knees with her fists, but her brother persevered.

"A light has come on in the weaponry room," Rosemary reported, her voice a fever pitch. "Run Gabriel. It's your last chance. Run to the end of the gardens and climb onto the greenhouse roof. It's a bit of a jump but you'll make it to the other side!"

"No! He can't go! He's mine," Floriana screamed, taking only a second to wonder why Rosemary had called him by a different name.

"Run! RUN!" Rosemary yelled.

Gabriel backed away, almost tripping over his own feet.

Delwyn had unintentionally slid back down the gate a few inches, in amidst all the shouting, but continued on his quest to reach his sister.

"COME BACK!" Floriana cried to Gabriel.

"RUN!" Rosemary encouraged him.

She did not see her sister reach for an arrow from her quiver –

Didn't see her pull back the string of her bow and aim –

The only thing she saw was a slither of a shadow ripping through the moonlight and tearing into the flesh of the boy's right calf.

"NO!"

Gabriel hit the gravel path face first. He rolled onto his back howling at the moon. He touched the arrow protruding from his leg and thought he might vomit from the pain of it.

"What were you thinking?" Rosemary snatched Floriana's bow from her, just as their brother fell to the ground on their side of the fence. He was on his back like a struggling tortoise, winded, and yet still starry eyed with love.

"Look what you made me do!" Floriana huffed. "The boy never would have run away if you hadn't got involved. It's all your fault I had to do this, Rose."

"No, no," she whined, peering through the bars at Gabriel bunched up awkwardly on the ground.

When Miriam and Elanor suddenly marched from the shadows to find the four of them in different states of bloodiness, pain and anguish, their mouth's dropped open in unison.

"Miriam," Rosemary called, as the knight used the key about her neck to open the front gates. "Oh, Miriam, please listen to me. I beg you." She latched onto the knight's armour as soon as she could reach her, and between weeping, explained, "the boy is with us. He means no harm at all, I swear it. We've had an accident. A game gone very wrong. Don't tell my father. Please. *Please*."

Floriana's teeth were gritted together and her lips firmly sealed as she observed her sister. She then passed through the open gate, stepped over her winded brother, (who tried to grab onto her gown on passing) and made her way over to Gabriel.

"Does it hurt?" she bent over and asked him.

Gabriel had closed his eyes to her, but nodded madly.

"My sister is protecting you again."

He said nothing.

"I won't stop her."

Floriana stood up straight as Elanor came to her side. "He's injured," she said. "Take him to the healing wing."

"Who is he?"

"My brother's friend," she lied. "Delwyn sneaked out for a beer at the pub and brought him back here. Don't judge my brother for the company he keeps. They're both foolish boys."

Elanor frowned at Floriana, but had no time to further question her. The Prince had found his feet and was running full pelt at his sister, his arms stretched out in front of him.

Miriam snapped to attention and wrestled him to the ground. His cheek hit the flower bed, which lined the gravel pathway. When he looked up, there was mud in his winning smile. The fall did not seem to bother him, because he was that much closer to the one he loved.

"You'll have to lock him away for a few days until the curse wears off," Floriana instructed coolly. "Keep him under permanent guard in his chambers."

The knights nodded, grabbing a hold of each one of Delwyn's arms.

"We'll send maids to carry the boy to the healing wing," Elanor said.

"Oh, my poor brother," Rosemary choked out, touching his face. It had been years since she'd seen his eyes.

He stared back at her, captivated by her features for a heartbeat, and then roared Floriana's name at the stars.

Chapter 22

Gabriel's eyes seared with pain as he opened them. Where he was, he had no idea. His head hurt. His skin was slick with sweat. He smelt like he hadn't bathed properly in weeks and his calf sang with pain beneath a bandage he didn't remember being put there.

"Where am I?" he asked the room.

He tried lifting his head from a pillow full of duck feathers, but it felt too heavy for his neck to support. He turned it to his left instead and saw a vacant wooden stool at his bedside.

"Hello?"

He was in a small room with no windows. There were two flaming torches in sconces and a simple hole in the stone wall – too small to squeeze out of – to provide some ventilation.

His eyes drooped.

He slept.

The second time he woke, he was immediately aware of his hand encapsulated by another.

"Gabriel?" came a hopeful whisper. "Are you awake? I can feel you stirring –"

He found the strength to turn and examine his visitor and was astonished to find a beautiful young woman at his side, clothed in a fine gown of fuchsia silk. She looked radiant, with her long brown hair tumbling around her, adorned with a silver tiara. Her posture was perfectly elegant and her eyes – well, he couldn't see them for they were bound beneath a gold scarf.

"Rosemary?" he croaked.

"You sound thirsty. Shall I send for water?"

"In a bit," he said. "What happened? I remember running and then, just pain."

"My sister pierced you in the leg with an arrow."

"Was she trying to kill me?" He breathed raggedly in surprise.

"No. Just stop you anyway she could."

"She didn't have to be so brutal about it."

"She only knows pain and violence. She's an odd girl, as you've probably guessed."

Gabriel squeezed her hand. "Does your father know I'm here?"

"No. Of course not!"

"Have I been sleeping long?"

"Long enough for the maids to get the arrow out and stitch you up. They say you've been a bit delirious for a few days now. Talking in your sleep."

"Days?!" he cried, straining his voice .

She nodded timidly. "You'll heal faster with rest."

"I need to tell Annabel where I am!" He shifted in the bed, trying to get up. Rosemary stood up, reaching blindly for the bed. She patted the mattress and seated herself beside him, placing a hand on his chest.

"Don't move. Your wound got infected. The

maids have been cleaning it every few hours."

"Please, it's important she knows –"

"Who is she?" Rosemary cut in. "If you don't mind me asking."

"A girl," he said, cautiously. "A young girl. I've been caring for her."

"And she's all alone?"

"No. I befriended a local woman. Seren her name is. I'm hoping she's still watching over her."

Rosemary thought about his. "I will go to them for you."

"Really?"

"Certainly. I could do with a stretch outside the palace."

Gabriel sighed. "Thank you. Thank you so much."

She smiled and felt Gabriel shifting beneath her. He weakly lifted an arm and placed his hand under her porcelain coloured chin. A blush rose to her cheeks and she leaned forward slowly.

Gabriel's chest fluttered and his eyes felt dry. He couldn't blink. He couldn't stop the floating sensation in his limbs. He didn't question the severity of what he was about to do to someone cursed by black magic.

"Gabriel," she whispered, just as his lips found hers.

He cupped her face and placed his other hand on her waist, stroking the silk of her dress as she responded to his kiss.

When she pulled away, they listened contentedly to the sound of each other's breathing. They smiled until giggles rippled from inside them.

Gabriel's skin was on fire, but he felt okay. His feelings were real, not an influence of witchcraft, he was sure.

Rosemary's giggles died away and she began twiddling her fingers nervously.

"What's wrong?" he asked, reaching out to hold them still.

"This is so wrong," she admitted sadly. "My sister thinks she's in love with you."

Gabriel didn't stop to think about his words. "I would rather die than marry her."

Rosemary's head sunk in shame. "I know. She's cruel. But she is still my sister-"

"We've done nothing wrong here. Have we?" He looked at her for some assurance everything was okay, but deep down, he knew it wasn't. Not at all. She couldn't see his face right then and he couldn't look into her eyes.

"Delwyn is better," she said, quickly changing the subject to break an impending silence. "He fell under the curse. It lasted four days. He didn't hurt anyone."

"I'm sorry."

"Don't be. It's not your fault you got caught up in all this."

He pictured Annabel at Seren's hut, worrying. He pictured his maker, stalking through the streets of his world waiting for his return. He thought about all the people he'd bitten, the blood he'd drank and the sleepless nights he'd trudged through towns, drenched by rain. And then he thought about the sound of Rosemary's voice; the clarity of each soft word. He looked at her hair now and thought it beautiful; her skin too. He looked at her dress, the kind he'd never seen worn by the women in his world and how it made her look like some sort of angel.

"I'm not sorry I met you, though."

Her stern and troubled face wilted and her smile reappeared. She leant forwards again for a second touch of his lips, but the sound of the door opening on creaking hinges startled her and she jumped up from the bed.

"Princess?"

"He's awake!" she proclaimed, a little too loudly.

The maid, an old wizened woman with short hair pinned back from her face, entered bearing a bowl of water with a sponge floating in it. She nodded and shuffled around the bed, touching Gabriel's forehead.

"The fever is subsiding."

"I feel a lot better," he said.

"I'll leave you to it," Rosemary curtsied and reached out for a hand to hold. The maid lowered the bowl to the stool and took it quickly, guiding the Princess to the open door. "Gabriel, where might I find your...er...family?"

"A hut. On the outskirts. There's a lane that leads from the palace all the way around the outside, past farms and houses. She's the last hut. Usually has a fire outside and a pot of something on the go."

"Right."

"Just ask for Seren. People seem to notice her about the market from what I've heard from Annabel."

Rosemary nodded and cautiously exited the room.

When the door was closed behind her, she untied her blindfold and made her way to the front gates of the palace.

*

Annabel had shed many tears in Gabriel's absence. Accepting the fact he would not return, she had settled into a routine of helping Seren tend to her vegetables, washing clothes at the river, kneading dough to make bread and other house-hold duties like sweeping and dusting. She didn't enjoy one moment of it, but it was a distraction – and distractions were exactly what she needed.

Seren was quiet a lot of the time. Annabel wasn't sure if this was because she wanted the little girl to have space to mourn, or because she genuinely didn't like her being around. She hoped it wasn't the latter. Where else was there to go for an orphan child if Seren gave up on her?

"Seren?" Annabel tapped lightly on her bedroom door.

"Yes?"

"Do you need any help?"

The barefooted woman was stripping her bed, ready to take the blankets outside to beat the dust off and the sheets to the river for a good scrub.

"If you want."

Annabel reached over the large bed and picked up a pile of furs.

"Are you okay?" Seren asked, as the child paused.

Annabel looked lost in thought all of a sudden, staring at the wall.

"Sorry?" She focused on her.

"Are you feeling okay?"

"Not really."

Seren dumped her bundle back on the floor and advanced on her, pulling the girl to her body.

"I don't belong here, do I?" Annabel moaned into her hip.

"Well, you were dead once, right?" Seren replied, tweaking Annabel's nose in an attempt to cheer her up. "It'll take some getting used to, but in the end, you'll forget all about your past. That's if you want to of course."

"I'm not sure what I want. I never had to think about it before. Gabriel always made the decisions."

Seren patted the top of Annabel's head and then scooped up her pile of blankets and sheets once more, heading for the door. "I miss him too," she said. "I know we weren't aquainted very long, but it's been a long time since I had a man inside my hut. It was nice, to feel safe for a change."

Annabel nodded meakly.

"But we have to stop thinking…" Seren's words lingered on her tongue and were almost swallowed back down as her doorway was cast in shadow. She raced to the kitchen counter where a wooden cross crafted from two sticks lay and raised it towards the silhouette.

"What do you want?" she hissed, moving forwards purposefully. She tried her best to show no fear

"Forgive my intrusion, but are you Seren?" came

a sweet, uncertain voice. The stranger stepped into the room and the light from a nearby window cleared the shadows from about her face.

"Who's asking?"

"Princess Rosemary-"

"Princess *Rosemary*?"

"Yes, I-" She didn't get a chance to finish.

Seren dropped the cross to the floor with a clatter and with her raised hand, struck Rosemary across her perfect, pretty face.

Rosemary cried out in alarm, and clutched the stinging that spiked across her soft skin.

Annabel was speechless.

A burning hate had been revived in Seren's belly. The memory of her husband had hit her hard in that moment, when Rosemary had stated her name. She'd heard it so many times before from his lips. 'Rosemary will be mine when she comes of age.' He had shown no compassion for Seren; treating her more like a brat-sister than a wife.

"Why?" Rosemary trembled.

Seren was suddenly struck with guilt. It hadn't been Rosmary's fault that her husband had been so vile. She'd only been twelve years old at the time and none the wiser.

"Please forgive me, Princess," Seren said, with a slight stammer to her voice.

"She didn't mean it. We thought you were someone else," Annabel piped up, misunderstanding why Seren had done such a heinous act.

Rosemary was still stunned, stroking her cheek

and biting back tears.

"Sit down. Let me fetch you something to drink. Would you like a herbal tea?" Seren wondered, trying to clear the tension from the air.

"No...no...I came here with a message. It's from a friend of yours."

"Who?" Annabel burst out.

"Gabriel."

"He's alive?" Seren asked.

"Yes."

Annabel squealed with delight, twirled on the spot and lunged at Seren's waist, squeezing her tightly in celebration. She couldn't believe her ears. She was so happy, she thought she might explode.

"I'm glad to see this pleases you both," Rosemary said. "He's at the palace. He had an accident. An arrow went through his calf. But he's healing. He'll be able to leave soon, I should think."

"Can we see him?" Annabel asked in a breathless hurry.

Rosemary's face darkened. "I don't think it would be wise."

"Why not?" she whined.

"My father doesn't know he's there. We want it to be kept quiet, for his safety."

"How did he even get there in the first place?" Seren sank onto a stool. Something about this didn't seem to add up.

Rosemary sheepishly held her hands in front of her. "My sister brought him in."

"He was cursed?" Annabel asked.

"He can't have been. I checked in the dungeon. He wasn't there," Seren reminded the child.

"No. He was in her room."

"What? Why?" Seren frowned.

"I won't speak ill of my sister and I won't say anymore on the matter. What Gabriel chooses to tell you on his return is his doing. But for now, you know enough." She inclined her head and turned to leave.

"Do I have your word he's safe?"

"Of course."

"If he doesn't come back with both hands, I swear I'll start a war. Even if I'm the only one fighting."

Rosemary showed her acknowledgment of this threat with a flicker of worry across her face and then made her way to the door.

"He's alive," Annabel whispered to herself, twirling around once more. She felt as light as a feather.

Seren remained seated, her eyes narrowed to slits as she watched the Princess leave. This was wonderful news. Amazing even. Gabriel was safe! But in the presence of two cursed Princesses, it was hard to tell how long for.

Chapter 23

She came to him in the dead of night, quietly in slippers. Pressing down on the brass handle, she pulled open the door. Inside the room, with a single white candle at the bedside, she perched on the edge of his bed.

"Gabriel?"

"Rosemary?"

A soft chuckle came from her lips as he opened his eyes, only to snap them sharply closed again. He'd only seen her hands – fingernails short and bitten, with mud underneath them. This was *not* Rosemary.

"I bet you wish it was her, don't you? My saintly sister and her good intentions."

Gabriel felt panic rising. He turned his head towards the candlelight that flickered against his closed lids, making his darkness seem tinted with red.

"I had hoped to make my sister jealous, with you at my side. I never imagined that both of you would betray me."

"She didn't betray you. It was all my idea," he lied. "I threatened her until she swore she'd help me escape."

"You must think I'm a prized fool!" she snapped. "If you'd threatened her, my brother would have found out and burst into my bedchambers to put your head on a pole!"

His mouth went dry. He didn't doubt her one little bit.

"No. Rosemary likes you. That's what it all boils down to." She leant forward and stroked his midnight hair, moving his fringe back from his forehead. "And I suppose you have feelings for her too?"

Silence.

And then –

She reached out both hands, using her fingers to try and pry his eyelids apart.

"No!" he screamed. "Get off me!"

"Look at me!" she shouted. "LOOK AT ME!"

They struggled. Gabriel bucked, hoping to throw the Princess from him, but she was strong and managed to stay on the bed. She peeled his lids upwards and Gabriel's eyes rolled back in his head, so only the whites showed. It hurt him to hold them there, but at least he wasn't looking directly at her.

"Just look at me and this will all be over. We can be wed in secret and my father will have no choice but to accept it. The curse will never, ever wear off because you'll always be looking lovingly into my eyes! And we can live in our own little palace, away from my *perfect* sister."

"HELP!" Gabriel howled. He no longer cared about hiding from the King. He refused to fall under her spell.

"No one is coming for you," Floriana whispered in his ear. "I sent them all away."

"HELP!"

She slapped a hand over his mouth and used the other to continue prying his left eyelid open. Blood appeared where she'd pinched the flesh beneath her jagged, bitten nails.

"I can wait here all night," she said.

Gabriel wriggled a hand from beneath his blanket and hit the Princess in the side of the head, knocking her to the floor. She landed on her hip with a loud 'oof' and gripped her hip in discomfort. She pulled a tiny dagger from her ankle. Gabriel, unaware of this for his eyes were tightly closed, hissed in pain as she sliced the blade across his shoulder.

He fell to the floor, huddling himself in the corner of the room with his arms raised above his head in protection. He cried out at every wound that burst open with Floriana's swooping weapon. Blood dripped down his forearms in thick streams.

"HELP!" he yelled again, between sobs.

The door opened and the cutting stopped.

"Flo!" Rosemary exclaimed. She was in her night gown and slippers also, bearing an apple in one hand and a honey cake in the other. "What are you doing?!"

Floriana dropped the knife. She looked at the mess of blood over Gabriel and then stormed from the room, without a single word in her defense; running through the corridors with tears of rage in her eyes. When she reached her bedchamber, she slammed the door as hard as she could, waking the sleeping knight outside.

"Gabriel!" Rosemary fell to her knees, dropping the apple and cake to touch the boy gently on the shoulder. She wasn't blindfolded and quickly told him so. "Don't open your eyes. Lean on me. I'll guide you to the bed."

He fell awkwardly onto the mattress, the flesh of his arms sliced to ribbons.

"I'll send for help. We need to stop the blood flow."

"Annabel, did you see her?" he wheezed.

"Yes. Yes! They know you're here." She ripped the sleeves from her nightgown and wound them around the worse wounds on each of his arms. With his head against the pillow, she could see a nasty cut on his cheek also.

"She's mad," Gabriel murmured through the pain.

"I didn't think she'd come for you. I'm so sorry."

"Rosemary. I think I should leave. Soon."

"You can't, not like this." She tried to wipe the blood from his face with her fingers, but more oozed from the cut.

"Bandage me up, and take me to the gates. Please Rosemary. She'll come back for me if you don't."

Rosemary chewed on her bottom lip. She looked at Gabriel's trembling body and his stained bed sheets. The knife lay on the floor.

"I'll send for a maid to wrap you up properly."

Gabriel reached out and touched her arm. "I really wish things could be different," he said.

She gently kissed the top of his hand. "I know."

When Gabriel's wounds were cleaned and patched up – some of which needed to be stitched before they were bandaged – Rosemary carefully supported him all the way to the main front gate, where the knights watched them both suspiciously.

"I'll see you again," Rosemary promised. "Those stitches will need to be removed at some point."

"I won't be here much longer," he informed her, solemnly.

"Where are you going?"

"Home."

"We can still meet, surely?"

"It's not...it's not a place you can reach easily."

She frowned. "Just say it Gabriel. You don't want to see me anymore."

"No! I promise, it isn't that. It's just... well... I'm not exactly from this world."

She laughed. "Next you'll tell me you're not even human!"

"I wasn't," he sighed reluctantly. "I was...something else. And then I came here through a mirror. It changed me."

"A mirror?"

"If I don't bring back a worthy husband to my..." He stopped himself and tried a different angle. "...to a monster back home...she's going to kill me. She sent me here, to find her a man."

"This sounds all rather bizarre to me-" she complained.

"So do cursed Princesses and marshes filled with severed hands. Life *is* bizarre."

Rosemary closed her mouth and slowly nodded.

"I'll stay for a few more days, but then I must leave and face her. Better to face the enemy on familiar ground than bring more evil to this Kingdom."

Rosemary touched his face. "You are a brave boy. I can tell."

"I try to be."

"And whatever you are back home, I would still like you just the same."

He blushed, thinking he very much doubted that.

Miriam marched over with the key to the gate in hand and nodded to the Princess on passing. The bars in the centre separated with a creak and Rosemary moved behind Gabriel's back. She untied the blindfold and stood up on her tiptoes.

"Count to ten. Then open your eyes and I'll be gone."

He inclined his head to the warmth of her breath against his ear. Her eyes filled with tears as he cupped her right cheek in his warm palm, kissing her on the lips.

"It's been an honour, Princess."

She smiled weakly and when he let go, she ran.

Chapter 24

The sunlight was waning. The maids had already been around to light the candles and stoke the fire, but Prince Delwyn hadn't moved from his bed. In his hand was a solid gold crown. It was smaller than his father's – and inferior in appearance – but it was his birth right. He'd only worn it once, as far as he could remember, when his sister's had received their little child sized tiara's of silver and crystal at a grand ceremony. Rosemary had been twelve. Floriana eleven. A year before the curse.

When there came a knock at the door, Delwyn assumed it was another maid. They'd been worrying around him for days. He vaguely remembered being under the curse, sickeningly thinking of strategies in which he could escape and reach Floriana. None had gone according to plan. He'd almost impaled himself on a rake one afternoon, which had been left on the earth below his balcony.

Now, his head throbbed with the aftermath of the spell. It had dissipated that morning, leaving him weary and embarrassed. Crawling into bed, he'd remained there for hours, getting up only to relieve his bladder.

"Delwyn?"

The voice that met his ears was gruff and male;

the only male voice besides his own that could be heard within palace walls.

"Father?" He sat up quickly, but felt a fuzziness in his head that stole his vision for a heartbeat.

"It's all right, son. Stay there. You don't have to get up."

The King entered the room with a curt nod to his maid, Emily, who closed the door obediently behind him. He was in his usual purple robes, with the white trim around the sleeves and collar. His hair looked thinner on top beneath his wonderous crown of many jewels.

"Pray, tell me. How did this happen?"

Delwyn shrunk under his covers. He felt like a small boy again, not the man who'd slayed a wolfman and mounted its head on his father's wall as a gift.

"A mistake, Father. One that I've paid for."

The King grunted and sat on the bed. "I can see that. What were you all doing out so late? Should I be concerned that my daughters – the ones we are obliged to love and protect unconditionally – are out in the woods in the dead of night?" His face reddened. "And that my son and heir to the throne is *supposedly* sneaking off with boys to drink ale in dirty pubs?"

The Prince's hands were sweating, leaving a trail of moisture on his crown, which he continued to fondle.

"These stories that have met my ears in recent days have deeply upset me, boy."

Delwyn bit the skin inside his mouth nervously.

"But it's also made me realise, you are a man and a man will do what he wishes – even if he is of royal blood."

"Father, I'm so sorry. I never meant for it to get out of hand. We had no idea that Flo' and Rose were wandering in the woods," he lied quickly. "If I had, I would have scolded them myself."

"That's not for you to bother with. It is my duty as a parent to punish them. I came here to apologise for being so wrapped up in my own misery that I can't bear to witness you all growing up."

"Mother would understand –"

The King put his head in his hands, an act that Delwyn had never witnessed before. His father usually sat so straight, even for an old man with a bad leg.

"No. She'd be ashamed of me. Of everything I do."

Delwyn did not try to dissuade him from this because he was right; she would have been ashamed of him if she were still alive.

"That being said, I can't change. Not entirely. I've made a name for myself here. I am a King to be feared and I relish in that."

"Yes, father," Delwyn nodded in understanding because he believed it was expected of him as a loyal son.

"I will continue to take the hands of those who are stupid enough to look at my little girl's faces."

Panic rose in the Prince's chest suddenly. Was his father implying that he would take his son's hand for being so careless that night by the gates? Surely not?

"I have every faith in you, that you will make a great King one day, boy."

"Yes, Father," he replied meekly, the sweat visible on his brow now.

"And the curse is punishment enough for you, so do not worry. I won't be so cruel to my own flesh and blood."

He sighed in relief.

"I want to tighten security, however. Bring in more knights. Train them. That will be your new challenge."

"I'll get right on it."

"I don't want my daughters wandering around at night anymore either. If anyone should see them out of their chambers past eleven, I want to be told."

"Of course."

"And I don't want you going to pubs. If you want a pint of ale so badly, nothing's stopping you from joining your old man in the dining hall for a few." He tried to smile but it didn't look right on his old and wrinkled face.

"Understood."

"Good. Now get up and stop acting sorry for yourself."

"Yes, Father."

"If you make a habit of it, you'll end up like me."

Delwyn watched his father reach out a hand and clasp the inferior crown between his fingers. He then raised it and put it on his son's head.

"There. Where it belongs."

Delwyn smiled.

"A handsome boy such as yourself should be thinking about finding a wife soon."

"Mother would have hated anyone I brought home," he admitted.

"Yes, well a mother will always judge any woman her son chooses to spend his life with. But I for one miss the company of a female. I know what it's like. All I'm saying is keep your eyes open. There must be someone around that takes your fancy."

Delwyn considered this. He rarely left the confines of the palace. And he wasn't likely to marry a maid. He was always too busy or wrapped up in his own thoughts to even think about women.

"Yes, Father," he said, courteously.

The King patted Delwyn's forearm and stood up. When he'd left, Delwyn lay back down against his many pillows in thought. He felt better for a short while, until the familiar tendrils of shame coiled up his spine. Unexpectedly, he threw his crown across the room, where it hit a candle off the table. The flame sputtered out before it could do any damage and Delwyn rolled over, pulling the blankets over his head.

*

Rosemary swished her paintbrush backwards and forwards over the page, one hand propped under her chin. She was in a dismal and despairing mood again, pining for the only boy she'd ever liked.

She thought about the conversation they'd shared before she'd left him at the gate. Something about an enemy, a mirror and being something other than human. It made her pulse race. So much danger surrounded him. It was a sure-way for her to wind up hurt, but she couldn't stop herself from wanting him deeply, with

211

every fibre of her cursed being.

"Oh Gabriel!" she moaned, thumping down her brush and splattering paint all over the page. It wasn't her finest work anyway. The black mess on the page was supposed to resemble his face in the moonlight, but she had thrown an inner tantrum at the fact she hadn't seen his eyes. "Stupid curse," she growled. "Stupid witch! Why'd she curse us anyway?"

She walked to the window, with its low, cushioned ledge and sat down. She could hear her songbird in the neighbouring room, trilling a beautiful tune from the balcony. It soothed her as she closed her eyes and tried to forget. But Gabriel's voice filled her head. She could see his midnight hair overhanging the blindfold about his eyes. And his perfect kiss registered on her lips as if a phantom was touching her.

"Men," she breathed, painfully. It was an inner pain, in her chest. It triggered something in her eyes and sent tears flowing, heavy and fast. "I want him back," she sobbed into her knees.

An hour later, after mopping her face with an embroidered handkerchief, she decidedly left her chambers in pursuit of the only person who really understood her.

On her travels, a maid had warned Rosemary of Delwyn's state of mind. He was incoherent as far as anyone could report and had been sleeping long, long hours.

"He'll make himself ill," a maid called Kira intoned. "Maybe you can talk some sense into him."

Rosemary had agreed that she would try.

"Brother?" she whispered into the room. "Are you awake?"

"Go away," he grumped from his bed. Usually, he would rush to her aid and guide her safely to a chair or settee. Instead, he watched her bump her shin into the table, from beneath the safety of his blankets.

"Ouch," she exclaimed, rubbing her skin. "Where are you?"

"The bed. To your right."

She turned in the direction of his voice and decided it was better to stay fixed in one spot, if he was going to refuse helping her.

"What do you want, Rose?"

She was taken aback by his tone. He sounded as depressed as she felt.

"I...I just wanted to talk to you."

"I'm not in a talking mood. Why don't you speak to Flo' if you're bored?"

"She won't talk to me. She's locked herself away in her bedroom and won't come out. She specifically stated no visitors. Plus, I'm not entirely pleased with the way she dealt with matters that night with Gabriel —" His name almost stuck in her throat.

"Neither am I. But it's over now."

"Are you all right?"

"Do I sound it?"

"Why are you so sad? You did nothing wrong-"

"I should have been more careful. I failed again."

"No, you didn't."

He slapped his arms down against the top blanket and heaved a great, audible sigh. Rosemary was moving from one foot to the other anxiously. She looked lost and alone, with the blindfold around her pretty eyes. He pitied her in that moment, standing at an incorrect angle to his bed.

"Come here." He threw off the covers and walked to her, taking her by the hand. "Sit down."

"Thank you," she said quietly.

Sitting cross-legged on her brother's bed, she informed Delwyn of Floriana's madness; cutting Gabriel's arms to ribbons. She timidly shared with him that they'd kissed on many occasions and that he had left because he was a wanted man.

"I have such a huge hole in my heart," she sniffed. "And it just keeps getting bigger."

"Do you...love him?" Delwyn asked.

Rosemary hesitated. "I have goose bumps when I'm near him."

"Yes, but do you love him?"

She nodded. "I think I do, yes. I'm not sure. I've never loved anyone before."

"Me neither," he exhaled slowly.

"The thought of never seeing him again is killing me inside."

Delwyn stared at the wall and Rosemary staring at the darkness. "Maybe I could help."

Chapter 25

Annabel hadn't quit smiling, from the moment Gabriel had stepped through the open doorway of the hut. He'd stopped momentarily to admire the circle of salt and herbs surrounding it and she'd run head first into his belly, winding him. She crushed him under her arms as if he might disappear again if she let go.

Seren had approached him too, with an expression that was hard to read. She lifted her arms and enclosed him in them, squashing the little girl between them in a group hug that lasted a good few minutes.

Gabriel rotated between laughter and wincing. His neatly bandaged arms had showed signs of blood seeping through with all the activity, and on realising this, Seren had led him to the blankets.

There he stayed for two days, dipping in and out of sleep.

Every time he'd opened his eyes, either Seren or Annabel were present, mopping his brow with cold water.

"Sorry I can't chop wood for you," he said, smiling.

Seren moved her hand away and smiled back. "Don't worry, boy. I'm making note of how many labour hours you owe me."

She offered him stew that night, which he took graciously. He hadn't eaten properly for a long time now and his body was visibly thinning. His skin was pallid and his eyes had lost their sparkle.

"What's wrong?" Seren asked him, one night.

Annabel was lying on the bed of blankets next to him, asleep. She'd scooched up to him as close as was physically possibly, thumb in mouth and had fallen into a dreamless sleep faster than ever before. Since his return, she'd found peace – performing her chores in the day with a grin as big as a sunbathing cat's.

"You look completely defeated."

"I feel as if I am," he replied, stroking Annabel's hair.

Seren lifted her bottle of wine and took a swig. Her long brown hair was pushed back behind her shoulders and her nightgown dipped low enough to show the pronounced shape of her collar bones in the candle light.

"I won't ask what they did to you, but I will admit something. I know why you came here."

His eyes flared with surprise and a hint of embarrassment. "She told you?"

"She thought you'd died or worse, gone off without her."

"I see," he said, looking at the sleeping child.

"You will not find a man here to go with you."

"You're so sure of that?"

She averted her eyes. "They dream of better things, but they also fear the unknown."

"So you speak for every man?"

She gazed at him, the bottle of wine poised in her hand. She took another swig.

"You're right." He breathed out sharply. "I knew it from the moment I saw the hands in that bog. Just as I know I can't stay here much longer."

Seren lifted her eyebrows. "We can always come to some arrangement. You can stay here as long as you require a roof over your head. I'll help you-"

"No, no. She'll come for me anyway."

"She?"

"My maker."

"Ah, yes. You were a vampire, right?"

He nodded, waiting for her words of disapproval, but they never came.

"I won't let her kill Annabel," he said, with determination spiriting him. The stew had warmed his belly and he was feeling much stronger for it.

"I won't let her kill Annabel," he said, with determination spiriting him. The stew had warmed his belly and he was feeling much stronger for it.

"You're going?"

"Will you watch her for me?"

Seren and Gabriel stared at Annabel. She was smiling around the obstruction of her soggy thumb.

"Are you coming back?"

"If I survive this, of course I'll come back."

"And you're sure you have no choice?"

"I've never been terrified of anything," he said, "until I met my maker. She's death incarnate."

"Scarier than the Princesses?"

Gabriel blushed, thinking about Rosemary and her sweet kiss. "Much scarier."

Seren's head felt light and dizzy. The wine was getting to her, and her smiles became sloppy.

"Well, I'm going to love you and leave you boy. Tomorrow, I want to see you up and about. No more slacking." She pointed a finger at him.

"I will," he promised. "And thank you, for everything."

She winked and left the room, bumping a hip into the door frame on passing.

Gabriel laughed. Seren was amusing, but she was also right. He'd lingered long enough. It was time to meet his maker for one last time.

*

"Delwyn!" Seren cried, dropping her mug of herbal tea onto the ground outside her hut. She'd been nursing a pounding head after the previous night's wine slurping at Gabriel's bedside and couldn't believe her eyes as the prince approached. "I mean, Prince Delwyn."

She raked her fingertips through her wild locks of hair and patted down the layers of her skirts that had been bunched up around her ankles on the doorstep.

"Good morning," he nodded cheerfully. "Is this, by chance, the residence of Gabriel?"

"Um, temporary residence, yes," Seren stood up in his presence and quickly entered the hut. "Gabriel. You have a visitor. A royal visitor!" she called, eyeing the mess of egg and toast on the table and the blankets piled up by the wood burner.

Gabriel emerged from under his blanket, with his hair sticking up at odd angles. He had bags under his eyes and his bandage had unravelled on his right arm, revealing puckered pink flesh, stitched neatly.

"What happened?" the Prince questioned, as he entered behind Seren. He was dressed in a hooded brown robe, which he lowered from his head when he was safely out of sight from prying eyes.

"You mean this?" Gabriel rolled his sleeve over the wounds in embarrassment. "A mishap with a knife."

Delwyn fixed gazes with the boy. He read the word 'Floriana' in his eyes.

"I've come to speak with you."

"Take a seat," Seren encouraged, pulling out a stool. It scraped across the wooden floor, but he smiled in appreciation and sat down. Gabriel sat opposite and Seren lingered nearby, unsure of herself.

"You can stay," Delwyn said, settling her.

She sat at the table with them, hands neatly folded on her lap. She caught the Prince's eye. He was examining her wavy, flyaway strands that were falling over her forehead.

"Is the Princess okay?" Gabriel wondered.

"I assume you mean Rosemary?"

He nodded, colour blossoming in his cheeks.

"It is because of her that I'm here." He laid his hands out on the table in front of him. They were warm and pink from being confined to the pockets of his robes on the journey over. He'd left in a hurry, before his father could summon him and realise he was missing.

"I must be frank with you, boy. My sister is pining for you."

Seren cut a look at Gabriel, whose lips remained tightly sealed.

"She came to me last night and told me of your obstacle back home. The thing that keeps you from her."

"Forgive me for speaking out of turn, Prince Delwyn, but there are a great many things that will keep me from her. I have strong feelings for your sister, without a shadow of a doubt, but is there really any hope?"

"I believe there is."

Gabriel raised his eyebrows in surprise.

"You seem like a good hearted lad. And if I know Rosemary, she wouldn't have fallen for any man that wasn't worthy of her. And so, I'm offering my services."

"Services?"

"Yes. On one condition."

"I'm sorry, but I'm confused. What do you mean by services exactly?"

Delwyn looked from Gabriel, to Seren, and then back to Gabriel. "Well isn't it obvious? I will go with you to slay the beast that hunts you. And you, my friend, will help me hunt down the witch so that you can be with my sister without the difficulty of her cursed blood."

Seren opened her mouth to say something, then closed it sharpish.

"Delwyn, I don't think it would be safe for –"

"Don't underestimate me. I killed the wolfman."

"Yes, but your father might –"

"What my father thinks became of no concern to

me on the night my mother died. He told us to leave him alone and not to harrass him. We were children. We were scared and upset. We wanted someone to care for and love us… tell us everything would be okay."

The hurt in Delwyn's eyes flared before them and Seren felt compelled to reach out and lay a hand over his in comfort.

"I'm not sitting in my bedchambers waiting for his crown. I'm not going to send my knights out to do the jobs I should be doing for my people. I will NOT pace my room, knowing Rosemary and Floriana are prisoners too. I want change and I want it NOW."

"What if we can't find her? The witch I mean?"

Seren was reddening deeply. She chewed her bottom lip and gripped the Prince's hand even tighter.

"All I ask is your help and support in return for my own," the Prince bartered.

"Is your sword made of real silver?" Gabriel asked.

"Of course." He touched the hilt automatically, feeling the cool metal in his palm

"Good," he replied. "Because you're going to need it."

Chapter 26

"Tell my father, should he ask for me, that I've left for a few days."

Emily, the King's personal maid, nodded enthusiastically outside the doorway of the palace. She watched on in bewilderment as Delwyn mounted an awaiting stallion – its reins grasped steadily in the hands of Elanor.

"Are you sure you don't need assistance?" Elanor asked him, feeling unease at the sight of the Prince's full-battle armour. His father would be completely enraged by the knowledge that he'd left without his guard.

Delwyn took the reins and signalled to Miriam to unlock the front gates.

"I'll be okay," he assured her.

"Be safe, my Prince." Elanor bowed, and retired to her post at the front door, beside a watchful Emily.

He had not delayed. From Seren's little hut, he'd returned home to prepare, stopping only to tell Rosemary that Gabriel had agreed to his terms. She'd been elated, clapping her hands and then throwing herself at her brother so she could hug him.

*

At the hut, Gabriel stood in the doorway watching Seren leave with Annabel. He'd asked the bare footed woman to take the child to the river for a swim. He'd lied and told Annabel that he was well enough to chop wood again, and that she'd be bored if she hung around and watched.

"But I can help carry the wood to the pile!" she had insisted.

"Go and have some fun. You've been cooped up for days. Don't worry about me."

Before she'd gone, hand in hand with a dole-eyed Seren, he'd hugged Annabel as if it were the last time. She'd thought nothing of it, squeezing him back equally as hard and waving goodbye as she went.

"Are you ready?" Delwyn came galloping into view, his black stallion foaming at the mouth from exertion. Its hooves kicked up mud and stone as it halted. The Prince held out a hand, which Gabriel took. With their combined strength, he swung himself onto the stallion's back, wincing at the pain that shot through his tender calf.

"Sorry, but there were no other horses to spare. My knights are about to set out themselves, in search of new recruits. Since our mishap by the gates, my father wants to increase security."

"To keep people out, or to keep the Princesses in?" Gabriel asked in a flat voice.

Delwyn dug his heels in the stallion's sides and they were away, tearing through the woods in half the time it took Gabriel and Annabel to make it on foot. The trees jumped aside, waving their branches in disapproval and flowers squealed beneath the pounding of hooves.

Gabriel kept one hand on the stallion's flank and one on Delwyn's shoulder, until he near fell to his death. From that point onwards, he unashamedly clung to Delwyn's waist, keeping his eyes peeled for low branches and unwanted missiles (some of the trees grew accustomed to throwing acorns and concurs at them on passing).

At the marsh, Delwyn called the stallion to a standstill. He took off his helmet and gawped at the puffy, severed hands, giving off a putrid stench of decay.

"My gosh," he breathed. "Is this my father's doing?"

Gabriel gagged at the familiar sight as a whiff of foul smelling flesh carried on a breeze to his nostrils.

"The knights must not bury the hands. They toss them in the river. Or the sewers."

"And this is where they gather…"

Delwyn blinked. "I never knew."

"Well, I'm afraid our exit is out there, in the middle of it all."

Delwyn swallowed and slid his helmet back on. A purple plume of feathers on the crown shimmered and waved like the wings of a bird. He made a clicking noise and coaxed his stallion forwards into the boggy water.

The stallion inched forwards but whinnied in fear, taking two steps back.

"Come on, Grey-Shadow."

It bucked its head, this way and that, huffing in

discontent.

"Yah! Yah!" Delwyn shouted, kicking his heels in harder.

Grey-Shadow let out an almighty squeal and rose on its hind legs, sending Gabriel and Dewlyn rolling off backwards. They landed in a heap; Delwyn on top of Gabriel, flailing about in fear of being trod on.

"Stop!" Delwyn bellowed, as Grey-Shadow took off, cantering in the direction they'd come. Delwyn cursed.

"We can't go back and get him, there's no time."

"But what if there's something else in there?"

"Annabel and I were fine."

"What of diseases?"

Gabriel shrugged. "We survived."

Delwyn's fists clenched and released, clenched and released. "Fine. Let's get a move on." He took the first step into the brown liquid and stumbled. It was deeper than he'd thought, sinking up to his waist in muck. But on advancing, the unlevelled marsh bed rose until only his knees were immersed.

"Be prepared for dips and holcs," Gabriel advised, wading beside him.

They slogged their way through the disgusting hands until the moon came out and bugs played havoc with their faces. Insects bit their ears and cheeks, noses and necks, even though Delwyn was covered from head to toe in chain mail and armour.

"How are they doing this?" he complained, taking a glove off to scratch at his chin.

Gabriel was silent. He was moving keenly

forwards, which encouraged the Prince to keep a fast pace.

Many hours of wading later, they came across a hillock with a single tree sleeping in the dead of night.

"We're almost there," Gabriel announced, pointing at the tree.

Delwyn looked up and smiled. "Good. I need to shake the water from my boots."

They climbed onto the hillock with blatant relief, sighing and smiling and led on their backs amongst the fronds of grass. The tree creaked in the wind, but did not show any dislike towards its visitors.

The mirror was still there, tarnished and at a slant. It was just as Gabriel last saw it.

"So that's it?"

"Yes."

"And we go through it?"

His silence was answer enough for the Prince.

Delwyn raised his hand and stroked the surface, which rippled beneath his glove. "Extraordinary," he whispered.

"There's something I should probably tell you before we do this," Gabriel said. He was squeezing water out from his socks before putting them back on his wrinkled, wet feet. "You won't be yourself on the otherside."

"What do you mean?"

"When you go through, you'll be stronger, faster."

The Prince's eyes filled with alarm. "That's good, right?"

Gabriel nodded slowly.

"One more thing-" He paused and stared the Prince square in the eye, anticipating his reaction.

"Go on. Spit it out," Delwyn snapped.

"I'm afraid…," Gabriel continued. "You'll be dead."

Chapter 27

"Dead?"

"Yes."

"How do you mean exactly? How can we be stronger and faster if we're coffin-bound?" Delwyn shuddered at the thought.

"Ever heard of something called a *vampire?*"

"Soulless creatures that feast on blood? The stuff of fairy tales."

"You have witches and wolfmen, but you think vampires are nothing more than a fairy tale?"

The Prince suddenly became unsure of himself. He sighed and tapped a boot against the foot of the tree, banging mud off the sole.

"It's what I am," Gabriel told him. "It's what I truly am and have been...for hundreds of years."

Delwyn stared probingly at the boy. He noted the vein in his neck and the grazes on the boy's arms. He was as human as ever.

"And if we go through this mirror, it'll change us?"

"Yes."

"But you seem so alive."

"I'm not dead now."

Delwyn frowned. "I can come back, right?"

"Of course."

He glanced nervously at the mirror. "Fine. I'll take your word for it."

Gabriel raised a hand to the mottled glass. He looked skinnier in his reflection, and the colour that had returned in his rebirth had been lost during his recovery of countless wounds. He was as pallid as the moon again. Delwyn looked radiant in comparison. His hair beneath his helmet poked out slightly, healthy and sunkissed. His long legs were muscular and his shoulders broad. He was truly a knight in appearance, but was he fit for battle?

"Would you like to go first?"

The Prince hesitated. "I'll wait, if you don't mind. I want to observe your passage through."

Gabriel sucked in a deep breath and lifted his right leg, stepping through the glass as if it were nothing more than air. It rippled around him and swallowed him whole, sucking at his limbs and throwing him into a realm of bright colours.

On the other side, he was expelled in a small burst of energy that propelled him through the water. His unprecedented appearance in the lake scattered the giant fish.

Delwyn flanked the boy, holding his breath as he boldly passed through. His eyes were wide and unblinking and his chest spasmed with an unusual pain as he broke through the surface of the mirror on its opposite side.

With a mouthful of water, he rose, lashing his legs and feet about like a mad-man. His fingertips reached for the dappled sunlight above and he gasped as he made it to the top; pointlessly sucking in oxygen and spitting up mouthfuls of water.

"My stomach," he choked, gripping the chainmail around his abdomen, whilst kicking frantically to stay afloat. He clenched his teeth and felt a sharp prick in his lower lip. Blood pooled from two incisions and trailed down his chin. Letting go of his stomach, he brushed his fingers over his teeth. They were sharp and pointed, like the fangs of the wolfman that permanently snarled on his father's wall.

He turned to Gabriel.

The boy's mouth sported a set of glistening fangs also.

"We're dead?" Delwyn sought confirmation, but before Gabriel could answer him, something sharp gripped his leg and dragged him under.

The Prince thrashed about in desperation, catching a glimpse of a silver scaled fish chewing on his armour-clad leg. The pressure of the creature's teeth against the metal made the flesh of his calf feel as if it would burst.

Water gushed into his lungs, and yet he did not feel the need to breathe. In realisation of this, he awkwardly wrenched his sword from its sheath and thrust downwards through the murk. The point of the blade penetrated the fish's bulbous yellow eye, spewing blood into the lake. It instantly let go of the Prince and wiggled about in pain.

The fish showed no mercy. Shooting through the water with teeth bared hungrily, they tore their finned-fellow apart, sending scales floating like falling stars.

Delwyn swam to the surface and found Gabriel.

"Are you all right?" He'd lost his helmet in the fray and hair stuck to his head in an unattractive pile, making the strawberry blonde strands appear mousey brown.

"It near bit my leg off!"

"If it had been me it grabbed, it probably would have," Gabriel said, patting the Prince supportively on the back.

"My helmet has gone." He struggled to stay above water, with the weight of his sword in one hand. He reached down and attempted three times to sheath it before it found its place at his side. His armour was heavy, making his movements sluggish.

"Quickly before they try it again," Gabriel suggested, making his way smoothly to the bank in a breast stroke.

Delwyn moved as fast as his armour would allow, lagging behind the boy. But even though he was slower in comparison, he was still much faster than any human being.

"This is phenomenal," he said, touching his bottom lip with the tip of his tongue. The bleeding incisions had healed and his leg felt better already. His words came out in a lisp between his fangs, but Gabriel's words were far more pronounced.

"Do you feel a burning sensation in your gut?"

The Prince nodded. "Like I'm burning inside with no oil to keep it going."

"Exactly. That's the thirst. You need blood."

Delwyn cringed at the thought of drinking bodily fluids for supper. "Is there another way to survive?"

"No. But you can live on animal blood if you drink enough of it."

"Animal blood? Is that safe?"

"Hmm. It's easier than taking the life of a human."

"Hopefully we won't be here long enough for me to try either," Delwyn admonished, slumping to the floor.

"We should stay alert." Gabriel advised. "She said she could sense my presence anywhere in the world so she'll know I've come back by now." He fumbled beneath the waistcoat Seren had given him – a forgotten item from her parting husband – and pulled out two pointed wooden stakes that he'd crafted himself in the night.

"Here. Take one. Silver and wood can kill her."

Delwyn took the stake with a bewildered expression.

"Aim for her heart."

"Sounds to me like this maker doesn't have one."

Gabriel grunted in agreement.

"Keep your eyes open for Nightcrawlers too," he added. "They're viscious, hungry creatures that lurk on the outskirts of most towns and villages."

"What are they?"

"Vampires that haven't fed for a while."

"How can I tell them apart from humans?"

"Oh you'll know. Vampires mutate if they haven't eaten in a long while."

"Charming," the Prince murmured, and scanned

his surroundings.

The trees here seemed still and the sky was a strange blue colour. It was colder than it was back home and the air smelt sweeter somehow.

"Can't you call her –" Delwyn asked, but stopped dead when a massive cloud of dark, black smoke burst before them. He fell backwards on his grassy perch, and from there, quickly hid his stake in a pile of reeds.

The hooded figure, in an ebony gown had appeared before Gabriel, her back turned to the Prince. She was taller than he'd expected, but slight of frame as far as he could tell.

Gabriel stood dumbly mesmerised. A familiar cold and bony hand wrapped around his neck, reminding him she could squeeze him till his head popped clean off.

"Gabriel, my dear sweet boy. You've returned at last. I was beginning to think you'd forgotten all about me." The slippery hiss of the maker's voice licked his innards dry, increasing the burning in his belly. He needed blood and a madness for it was building.

When she turned, she let go of Gabriel's throat and lowered her hood. Delwyn let out a gasp as he saw her for the first time.

Red curls bounced around a beautiful face, but the curls seemed to sink unexpectedly downwards in a limp and lifeless fashion, greying before his very eyes. Her face shifted into that of an old man's and she let out a croak of rage.

"Not now!" she screeched, clawing at her face with long fingernails like talons.

She bent down, averted from the Prince's direct

view, trying to maintain the guise of the redheaded woman. Her wrinkled flesh stretched suddenly over high cheekbones and her hair bounced back up, red like the flames of hell.

"That's better," she whispered, snapping her spine up straight and walking towards Delwyn. She raised a hand to him in a friendly gesture. "You must be my future husband, yes?"

He took her hand, but in that moment, she yanked him towards her and twisted his arm behind his back.

The Prince struggled against her grip, but her strength was like nothing he'd ever encountered. His bones felt as if they might snap in two if he budged an inch. His eyes bugged out of his head in pain.

"Do you think I'm stupid?!" she screamed. "I know this man!"

Gabriel stood frozen in fear, his hands fanned out before him in an attempt to calm down his maker. He did not reach for his stake, in case she broke Delwyn's neck, but his fingers itched for a weapon he could use none the less.

"He is the Prince of the Black Kingdom."

The Black Kingdom? Was that its name? Gabriel wondered. He'd never thought to ask –

"I can't imagine you convinced this troubled young man to marry me? A Prince of thieves perhaps would have come if you'd offered him riches, but a Prince of royal blood would have *never* left the palace for a stranger, unless he wished me harm."

"You're mistaken," Delwyn wheezed breathlessly. "I came for you because I wish to take a worthy bride."

"Hush," she spat, dragging him backwards through the grass. She stood on the bank, higher than Gabriel.

"You said you wanted a Prince and I brought you one," he reasoned with her. "I didn't fail you!"

"I was exaggerating," she laughed wickedly. "You didn't think I'd really expect you to find me someone of this social calibre? No! A real Prince! I'm actually rather impressed you convinced him to come, even if it was to trick me." She gave Delwyn's awkwardly folded arms a squeeze. "Now, he will die because of your insolence!"

She lowered her head faster than the naked eye could fathom and buried her teeth in the flesh of Delwyn's neck.

Gabriel ran at them both, tugging his stake free and brandishing it above his head.

The Prince's mouth opened in agony as the last of his human blood was sucked from his undead body, making his skin shrivel and tighten around his skeleton.

The maker made little noises of joy as she pulled a chunk of skin away from his neck. She then threw him to the floor, as Gabriel got too close for comfort. She jumped over Delwyn's body and darted for a tree, laughing when Gabriel caught her ankle mid-jump. He pulled her back down from the branches and her hysterical laughter increased as she hit the earth by her knee caps. It didn't slow her down however. She bounced up in an explosion of smokey black tendrils and dodged his reaching fingers.

One moment she was to Gabriel's left. The next she was to his right.

He couldn't quite figure out if she was moving faster than he could trace or if she could truly teleport, but all the while, her cackling laughter followed her in a ghostly roar.

"We made a deal and I kept it. I want my father's watch back and Annabel's pendant."

His maker appeared before him, her dead-set eyes becoming like bottomless pits. She looked haggard and weak for a moment, trying to grasp onto her guise as a young, voluptuous woman.

"You should have done as I asked of you," she barked.

"I did! I brought you a Prince," he argued.

They looked at Delwyn, who lay on his back in the grass, blood pumping from the wound at his neck. It was healing over slowly, but still, his vampire body could not withstand the draining it had taken.

"He wanted to marry you!"

His maker slapped him hard across the cheek.

"Liar."

"He did, I swear it." He clutched his cheek with one hand and with the other, quickly raised the stake.

His maker grabbed his wrist and pinched his skin until her fingernails penetrated his flesh.

The stake remained in his hand, just about, but she was twisting his arm until the point of the stake was aimed at his own chest.

"No," he begged. "Please!"

Her black, soulless eyes flashed with a bright

intensity that could rival the suns. She showed her grimy teeth, stained with age and smiled through her effort to keep Gabriel's weapon at bay.

The tip of the stake punctured his chest by an inch and a cry of pain ripped from his mouth.

His hands were shaking with the determination to keep it from finding his heart.

And then –

She let go.

Her arms fell to her sides uselessly and she glared at Gabriel in complete astonishment.

He threw the stake away, touching the small hole in his flesh. He looked back up at his maker.

From her own chest, there was an arrow, tipped red with blood.

She stared down at it, touched the point that had sliced through her unbeating heart and let out a gasp.

Suddenly, her body exploded; black smoke soaring into the sky and rushing over the lake in all directions.

The blast knocked Gabriel off his feet. He stayed down, lifting a hand to shield his face from the falling embers of his maker's dying flesh.

And when the smoke dispersed and the embers fell like snow all around him, he spotted in the distance, a boy holding a crossbow.

Chapter 28

"Eli! Is that you?" Gabriel projected through cupped hands.

The stranger made his way forward, lowering his bow to his side. The copper strands of his hair reflected the winter light. He was sure-footed and swift, keeping vigilant for other predators, but showing signs of a smile at the corner of his lips.

"So you came back? I knew you would!" Eli clocked Gabriel on the arm with a gentle punch, before noticing the Prince in the grass. "Oh gosh. He doesn't look as if he'll make it."

Gabriel rushed to Delwyn's aid, biting his wrist hurriedly and letting a quick stream of blood flow between the gap in the Prince's parted lips. Eli joined Gabriel's side, puzzling over the strangers face. He did not recognise the injured man.

"Another vampire?"

"It's hard to explain," Gabriel mumbled, supporting the Prince by the neck with the back of his hand.

Delwyn let out a dry cough that sputtered Gabriel's blood all over his chin. He then continued to suck at the wound, tasting the salty fluid running thickly down his throat. If he hadn't been in so much pain, he would have been disgusted with himself; drinking from a friend in order to survive.

"I've been coming back here every day since you disappeared," Eli explained, while Gabriel worked. "When I saw you were in trouble, I just reacted automatically."

"And a good job you did. I can't thank you enough."

Eli accepted the vampire's gratitude with a nod.

"This is no use," Gabriel announced suddenly. "I have to take him back."

"Back where?"

"Through the mirror. In the lake."

"I'm coming with you this time."

Gabriel looked up and gave Eli an uneasy glare. "It's not safe. You're better off staying here with your Pa'."

"He threw me out," Eli told him in a breathless rush. "They figured it was me who let you go. He tossed me out with no money for food or clothes for my back and I've been sleeping in the hay shed with the donkeys. Please, take me away from this place! I can't stay here anymore."

Gabriel grabbed a moaning Delwyn by his boots and began dragging him through the grass to the lake. He didn't have time to discuss recruiting another member of his 'team', even if they had just saved his life. But how was he supposed to stop the boy?

"It's deep. Your human lungs won't be able to make it."

"I'll die trying," Eli said.

The Prince let out another moan and reached out to Gabriel. "It burns. It burns so much."

"I know. We'll get you back home and you'll be strong again, I'm sure of it."

"Wait!" Eli called. He'd been stomping through the grass alongside the vampires and had come across something shining at his feet. "I think you dropped these." He picked up two chains; one bearing a small jeweled pendant and the other, much thicker, supporting a pocket watch.

Gabriel took the objects and clutched them to his chest. His luck was finally changing. He tucked them out of sight, content in knowing they were on his person at last.

"Did I do well?" Eli asked, dropping his crossbow to the ground. He didn't want to be burdened with a weapon whilst swimming.

"You did," Gabriel praised, and then slipped into the water backwards, with a mumbling and incoherent Prince Delwyn in tow.

Eli splashed into the lake after them, observing how Gabriel manouvered and then supported Delwyn by his chin, swimming out to the lake's centre. He then stopped moving all together, sinking like a stone to the muddy bed below.

Eli drew in the deepest breath he could manage, panicked that it wasn't enough, then exhaled and tried once more. He dived under, bubbles fluttering from the corners of his mouth and nose as he followed Gabriel and Delwyn's shadows through the water.

The giant fish circled them, but did not attack. They recognised the Prince's sword sheathed at his side and steered clear of it.

Delwyn's eyes fluttered and his energy waned. But in the moment he and Gabriel passed through the mirror, his brain felt as if it had been dunked into a bucket of ice. Eyes wild and hands flailing, he gripped onto Gabriel's hand as tight as he could. He could feel the sinewy flesh of his vampire body rapidly spreading to cover the hole in his neck and then with a pounding like a drum, his heartbeat reverberated inside his chest. The green sky of his own world met his blurry vision and from his lungs came the expelling of carbon dioxide.

He silently rejoiced as he felt the hillock beneath his legs.

"How do you feel? Are you still weak?" Gabriel tapped the Prince's cheek roughly. "Focus, Delwyn. Can you hear me?"

Delwyn located the boy with his eyes and managed a meagre smile. "We made it."

"We did," Gabriel smiled back.

Just then, the mirror rippled and spewed forth another figure, dripping wet and coughing up dirty lake water on his hands and knees.

"Who's that?" Delwyn rasped, in puzzlement.

"The kid that saved us."

"I'm not a kid," Eli snapped and as he lifted his head, two long fangs became visible. "What?" he demanded of the two males staring back at him. His words were tinted with a lisp.

"I'm sorry Eli, but there's something you should

know..."

The boy pricked his tongue against a fang and let out a cry. "What's happened to me? Why do I have fangs? Why aren't I breathing?" Panic spread through him like wildfire and he tried to physically pull the fangs from his gums.

"If you want to live in this world, I'm afraid you'll have to stay like that."

"You bit me! You bit me when I wasn't looking!"

Gabriel scowled. "You're being ridiculous. You know that isn't true."

"Then what are these?" He pointed at his teeth.

"If you enter the mirror alive, you'll be dead on the other side. And vice versa. Look at me. I'm human again."

Eli stood up and scrutinised the two males with his enhanced vampire vision. He could see fluttering pulses and juicy veins in both their necks. He licked his lips.

"You'll have to learn to restrain yourself. Hunt animals, not people."

"I'll live forever now?" He patted his chest and felt muscles that hadn't been there before. He stroked his arms and noticed his biceps had got bigger.

Gabriel nodded.

Eli thought about this frightening fact. Forever was a long time.

"You can still go home if you want. But make up your mind. There isn't much time."

Gabriel trekked down the hillock a small ways and bent down. From the marsh, he located a rock, pushing away a severed hand that floated nearby.

"What's it to be? Life or death?"

Eli looked lost, glancing from the Prince to the boy with the slippery rock in his hand. He thought about his Pa' and his abandonment. He thought about his twin brother and how he'd leered spitefully and viciously at him when the villagers had thrown mouldy tomatoes his way. When he'd fallen in the mud, with rotten vegetables in his hair, his brother had turned his back on him.

"Choose," Gabriel prompted. His palm moist with marsh slime.

"Death," Eli whispered, walking away from the tree and seating himself at Delwyn's side.

"If you're sure," Gabriel said. With the rock in hand, he bashed away at the mirror's frame, watching it crack and splinter. When it had separated at its joints, the glass in its centre slipped free. It slithered to the ground like liquid silver, splashing against his feet.

Delwyn nodded his approval at Gabriel and patted Eli on the knee. "Welcome to my Kingdom," he said. "A cursed lad like yourself will be right at home here, I'm sure."

Chapter 29

The victor's returned home the following day, tired but proud.

Gabriel taught Eli how to immerse himself in the woods, patiently waiting for a passing deer to catch and drain. The boy was a fast learner and did not complain about the taste, for he had not sampled human blood to compare it to. Both Prince and boy had warned the vampire that should he lose control, they wouldn't think twice about staking him through the heart and ending him where he stood.

When Seren's hut came into view, with its trail of smoke waving from the chimney, they picked up the pace. Eli was the first to reach the door, but did not open it, for he was a stranger to these people and did not mean to scare them.

Gabriel didn't knock. He went straight ahead and opened the door, calling Annabel's name.

The little girl was at the table with Seren, learning how to weave fronds to make a basket they could use to collect herbs in.

"Gabriel!" she exclaimed, rushing to him.

He picked her up in his arms and swung her around.

"Don't ever do that to me again!" Annabel said, lacing her arms around his neck and hugging him. "When Seren said you'd gone, I almost went after you! She had to lock me in her room!"

Seren joined them and nodded, confirming this.

Gabriel placed her on the floor and pulled the pendant from his pocket.

Annabel's face lit up, following its swinging pattern with her gaze.

"She's dead?"

"Thanks to Eli."

Annabel and Seren looked over at the figure standing nervously in the doorway. He kept his eyes averted; a habit of his in the presence of ladies. His mouth was closed to cover his fangs.

"Ginger-nut! You found us."

He grimaced. "Um...Do I know you?"

"We've met," she grinned. "I was a ghost."

"A ghost?" He swallowed.

"Sure. Gabriel killed me and I haunted him. I was there the whole time when you followed us to the lake."

"I knew it!" he remarked. "I knew I could sense something. But how are you-?"

"The mirror." She cut in, with a shrug.

Delwyn walked passed Gabriel and Annabel's lovely reunion – his eyes fixed on Seren. She noticed his approach and lowered her head, her hands twisting in front of her anxiously.

"My Prince." She curtsied respectfully as he came to a standstill.

"Seren-"

She looked up into his blue eyes and felt a jolt of adrenaline. Her skin was burning with heat.

He laced a hand around her waist suddenly, dipped her low and planted a kiss on her lips.

Annabel whooped.

Seren was dizzy when she came up for air.

Delwyn attentively brushed her long brown hair from her face and gave her a simple peck on her right cheek before parting.

"I'd better go," he said to his audience. "My sister will want to know we're safe."

Gabriel nodded in understanding, whilst bending down to help attach the pendant to Annabel's fragile, little neck. She wasn't making it easy – she kept bouncing up and down on the balls of her feet.

"Get some rest tonight. Tomorrow we'll rendezvous outside the palace gates. We have a witch to hunt. Eli, if you find yourself lacking in entertainment, feel free to join us. We could use your skills as a vampire."

"What? Vampire?" Annabel said, frowning at the copper-haired boy, who lingered nearby.

Seren heard the word vampire, but ignored it, lunging for the Prince's arm.

"Wait!"

Delwyn placed a hand over hers, where she'd gripped his armoured forearm. "I'll return for you," he promised.

"No, wait!" She looked pained. Her eyes were haunted. "I have...some information."

The room grew silent.

"What do you mean?" he asked, letting go of her hand.

"I mean..." She took a deep breath and fidgeted. Her voice wavered as she said, "I know...I know who the witch is that you seek."

They waited for her to continue.

A tear slipped down her cheek.

"Who is it?" Gabriel asked when the silence had dragged too long.

"She's been hiding in plain sight all along," she explained.

"Who has?" Delwyn demanded, his voice losing its patience and charm. "Who is it?"

Seren's eyes darted from Gabriel's to Delwyn's.

"My mother," she said.

Chapter 30

"You mean to tell me," Delwyn said, his brow furrowed and eyes fluttering, "That all this time…all these *years*…you knew who had cursed my sisters and you said *nothing*?"

Seren bowed her head remorsefully. "It's complicated."

"It was your duty to your King to tell him!"

"I know!" she cried, snapping her head up. "Don't you think I wanted to? The amount of times I went to the palace gates. The amount of times I approached you at the market! But I couldn't."

"Why?" he demanded.

"Because she's my mother! She's all I've got left!"

Annabel had found Gabriel's hand the moment voices had been raised and peered from behind his hip in bewilderment.

Delwyn roughly wiped the sweat from his face with his palm. "Tell me then…why did she feel the need to curse them at all? What had they done to her?"

Seren's cheeks burned red and her eyes flashed with shame.

"I went to her, as all troubled daughters would

have done, to the woman who bore them. My husband had left me because he was madly in love with Rosemary _"

"Your husband?" Delwyn interrupted.

"Yes. Do you remember the first time a man breeched the palace grounds and tried to get to your sister?"

"He got away from us."

She nodded.

"Did you help him escape?"

"To hell I did! I wanted to see him punished! He left me here all alone, broken inside with nothing but bits of his dirty laundry to remember him by."

"So you cursed my sisters?"

"*No.* I never meant for them to be harmed. It was my mother's doing. She acted without my consent. All I know is, I went to her in fits of tears and explained what he'd done to me and why. The next thing I know, she's conjured some sort of black spell and cursed both girls."

"But they did nothing wrong," Delwyn said.

"I know. I know," she said grimly, balling her hands into fists. "But my mother has a black heart. She was disappointed I'd married in the first place. I think she meant to punish everyone."

Delwyn slammed a fist down on the table. "All this time! I can't believe my ears. All this time you knew."

She reached out and grabbed his arm once more, but he recoiled from her touch. She looked pained by his disgust and wilted into a chair, her head in her hands. A soft sobbing came from beneath the veil of hair that shrouded her face and all those standing awkwardly by, looked on.

"If I take you to her, will you forgive me?" she asked, her face still hidden.

Gabriel looked to Delwyn for a reaction. Eli had no clue what this was all about and wisely kept his tongue still. And Annabel wanted to go over to Seren and comfort her, regardless of the woman's foolish secrets; she just did not like to see her friend in turmoil.

"Show me where she lives and maybe I'll think about it."

Now it was Seren's turn to be angry.

"How dare you!" she exclaimed. "How dare you judge me for protecting my own flesh and blood when you have done the exact same thing. Your sister tied up Gabriel! She tried to force him to love her! She put an arrow through his leg and cut him to pieces with a knife. If that's not evil, I don't know what is."

Delwyn turned his back on her, making to leave.

"But you'll never stop loving her will you? You'll never stop fighting for her, or protecting her?"

He paused.

"So you and I are no different!"

"Just tell me where she lives," he said quietly in defeat.

"Do you plan on going there now?" Gabriel asked incredulously. "We should at least rest first."

Delwyn rounded on Gabriel. "How can I rest knowing that witch is so close?"

Gabriel looked intently into the Prince's eyes, then over at Eli in the corner. "Well we're coming with you."

The tension broke and the Prince nodded. "Fine. I suggest you bring that axe outside with you."

Seren got up and walked towards them slowly. She was trembling from head to toe and her face was tear-streaked. "Will you do something for me if you get the chance?" she asked Gabriel, for she did not think the Prince would suffer to listen to her any longer. "Tell my mother I'm sorry. And that I love her."

Her watery eyes bore into his and all he could do was whisper, "Okay."

Then, she shared with the men her mother's location.

*

Prince Delwyn, Gabriel and new-vampire Eli stood outside the little cottage. It was familiar to Gabriel. He thought to himself how right Seren was; her mother had been hiding in plain sight all along.

The flowers shrank in fear as the axe in Gabriel's hand glinted in the last rays of sunlight. They also cowered before the Prince's silver sword that he grasped firmly in his right hand.

"Is this it?" Delwyn wondered aloud.

"This is it," concurred Gabriel. "And now it all makes sense."

The man he'd spoken to days before, with his two hands still intact, came to the door as the sound of the brass knocker, shaped like a fox, announced their presence. He looked cheery and well, his cheeks rosey and his teeth too white to be natural.

"May I help you?" he asked, frowning at them when he noticed the sword and axe.

Delwyn didn't wait for introductions. He raised his blade to the man's throat and forced him backwards into the cottage.

"Where is she?" he hissed.

"Gloria!" the man bellowed, his adam's apple bobbing up and down with each dry swallow. "Gloria, get in here!"

"What is it now, Daniel?" she called out of sight, from the room yonder.

The three boys stood in a line. Eli revealed his fangs to Daniel in a terrifying smile that made the man shiver involuntary.

While they waited for Gloria to arrive, Gabriel observed his surroundings. It was a typical old cottage with big wooden beams on the ceiling and rugs covering the floorboards. Her settee was old and patterned with flowers and under wooden ornaments (that had been carved by Daniel over the years), were off-white doyleys. Upon the mantel was a sketch of a younger Seren. Her hair was slightly shorter back then and her face, a little fuller. The picture had gathered dust, but you could still make out the happiness on Seren's face. She had been a beautiful child, as she was now a beautiful woman.

Daniel backed away from Delwyn's blade and fell into an armchair.

"What's the meaning of this?" he pleaded. "We've done nothing wrong."

"Daniel? Who are you talking to?"

Gloria emerged at last, her hands pink from washing dishes in a bucket out back. One hand grasped a hold of a walking stick, to assist her as she hobbled.

"My, my. Well if it isn't Prince Delwyn." Her wrinkled face darkened and her eyes went from brown to black. "I take it you're not here for a cup of tea?"

Delwyn stepped forwards, his arm aching from holding his sword aloft. But he held it there all the same, with adrenaline fuelling him every step of the way.

Gabriel glanced nervously at the Prince, waiting for some instruction. Was he going to ask the witch nicely to lift the curse or use brute force? On their walk along the lane, they had said nothing to one another about a plan of action.

"Witch!" Delwyn spat.

Her thin lips creased into a smile. "So you figured it out?"

"I was told."

"Ah, I see." Her eyes flickered with pain. "My daughter?"

Delwyn lifted the blade until its sharp tip pressed against the old woman's throat.

"I'm surprised she didn't tell you sooner. Always was a dreamer that girl. She said she wanted to be a white witch, until she realised her mother was a black one." She laughed. "And when she found out what I'd done, she never forgave me."

"Reverse it," Delwyn told her firmly.

Gabriel's hands sweated as he stood poised for action.

"I can't." She lifted her head in defiance. The curls of her thin grey hair brushed the blade at her throat.

"Reverse the spell *now*."

She smiled again. "Make me."

Delwyn clenched his teeth together and drew back his sword arm. In the moment it took him to bring the blade down at her shoulder, the old woman had vanished.

Daniel let out a scream that could rival a damsel in distress, curling up on the armchair with his hands on his head.

The three boys turned wildly about in search of her. As Gabriel was about to explore the back room, he felt his legs get knocked out from underneath him. The roof fell down on his head and the walls exploded. Stone and thatch flew in all directions.

Daniel remained in a huddle on the armchair, screaming hysterically and the boys floundered about in the wreckage, bruised and bloody.

"She's powerful," Delwyn wheezed, pushing rocks from his legs.

Gabriel lay beneath a beam. It crushed his middle and his eyes were full of dust and grit. Eli had been quick enough to dart away from the falling debris, thanks to his inhuman speed and helped lift the beam from Gabriel's body.

"She can't hide anymore, now that we know who she is."

"Quite right," came a voice from behind the Prince, as he clambered to his feet.

Gloria appeared from thin air and touched

Delwyn on the back of his neck. Where a handsome young man once stood, a frog replaced him, balanced on a plank of wood.

"Delwyn!" Gabriel yelled.

He made to grab the frog, but the Prince's little green amphibian body sprung into life, hopping towards the lane behind him.

"Where's he going?" Eli cried.

"Go get him," Gabriel instructed. "Don't let him out of your sight."

The vampire shot away, scooping the frog-prince up in his hands before it could disappear amongst the grass lining the road.

Gabriel located his axe and stomped over towards Daniel. The young man cowered and whined.

"I haven't done anything!"

Gabriel raised the axe, anticipating another visit from the witch. As he suspected, a split second before his axe met Daniel's skull, Gloria reappeared in a flurry of wind and sent a burst of energy at his ribs, knocking him sideways into the wreckage.

She laughed in amusement as he rasped in pain.

He was certain she'd cracked a few of his ribs.

Eli swooped down on the witch, his teeth bared; Delwyn-the-frog clutched to his chest. He caught her by surprise, but wasn't strong enough to hold her still. She threw the vampire from her back and sent him flying into what was left of her wall.

The frog-prince croaked in terror and slipped between Eli's fingers, bouncing off once more towards the lane. The vampire boy found his feet and went after the frog, avoiding the debris as best as he could.

Gabriel coughed up blood and gripped his side.

"I have no idea who you are," the witch growled from above him. "But I'll still have the utmost pleasure in killing you –"

"It's hard to believe you're Seren's mother," Gabriel spluttered, as the witch leant over him.

"Why's that?" she asked.

"Because she's so good and kind."

"Well, she gets that from her father's side. She doesn't know it, but I turned him into the wolfman that haunted the woods for years. The same wolfman that the Prince killed."

Gabriel was shocked by this bit of information. This woman was clearly insane. She'd caused so much pain and trouble. Her daughters own father had been slain by the Prince. If Gabriel ever survived this war, he decided he would keep it to himself.

"She told me to tell you something…," he whispered.

"What was that?"

"She told me to tell you…" He gripped his ribs and winced. The pain was immense.

"Be quick," she snapped.

"She's sorry and that she loves you."

"HA!" the witch laughed.

And in that brief moment her eyes closed and her head rolled back, Gabriel pulled a pouch of salt and herbs – that Seren had made for each of the boys before departing – and threw it into the witches face.

She let out a howl of pain as her eyeballs fizzled

in their sockets and her mouth frothed with white foam. She shrieked and clawed at her face. Her back twisted at unnatural angles. The walking stick was forgotten.

Gabriel dragged his axe from the rubble and stood up, ignoring the stabbing pains in his side. With a sure hand, he brought the axe down on the witches head.

She crumpled to the floor, becoming little more than a pile of rags…and a squealing mouse slipped out of one of the sleeves.

But Eli was quick off the mark, darting after her. He snatched up the Gloria-mouse, with her mouth still foaming, and snapped her neck in his hands.

"Got her!" he announced in triumph, just as the frog-Prince in his other hand became a human being once more. Weighed down by Delwyn's armour and body mass, he buckled under the strain and hit the floor.

Delwyn was disorientated and his skin had a slimy sheen to it. He was a strapping young lad of muscle and strength once more.

"Did we get her?" he asked breathlessly.

"We got her," Gabriel said.

The Prince felt tears pool in his eyes as relief flooded him. He ruffled the vampire's copper hair and pulled Gabriel down beside him, patting the boy on the back.

Gabriel smiled through the pain in his side and allowed his spirits to lift in celebration. He was free. The Princesses were free. The Kingdom was free.

"Um, excuse me chaps." Daniel walked unsteadily over to the three boys, sitting amongst the remains of the cottage. He looked down at them in

puzzlement, scratching his temple.
"Can someone tell me how I got here?"

Chapter 31

Eli walked with Seren to the place where the cottage once stood. She was clothed in black and wore a pair of onyx coloured shoes for a change, so that her feet weren't cut up by the debris.

Seren knelt down, picking up the broken body of the mouse in her hands.

Silently, she left Eli standing alone, making her way into the woods where she buried the mouse without a word, along with the photograph of herself as a child.

The rain began to fall. Her hair grew wet with the passing of minutes. When she was finished, she walked slowly back home, leaving her guilt behind her.

*

Gabriel was nervous. He was trying to cut the growth of stubble around his face with a knife from Seren's collection. On more than one occasion, he'd managed to nick his skin with the blade, causing blood flow, and reluctantly had to send Eli away, should he smell it.

"I've cleaned your shirt. Your trousers too," Seren informed him, eyeing up the boy in her x-husbands baggy old grey pyjamas.

Gabriel turned to Seren, who was lingering in the doorway of the hut. He was using the reflection in a bowl of water outside to manoeuvre the knife around his face.

"Let me," she sighed, stepping forward. With nimble fingers, she meticulously sheared the dark stubble off, revealing the pale milky skin of the human boy beneath it. "There. Cute as a button."

Gabriel smiled and rubbed a hand over his chin. "Thanks."

"Where's the vampire?"

"Hunting."

She made a grunting noise and folded her arms over her chest. "As much as I like Eli, he can't stay here."

"I know."

"I won't have him endangering any of us. One cut. One whiff of blood and he might attack."

"It's because he's new to it. He'll learn how to control it in time."

"I hope so," she muttered.

They entered the hut and Gabriel shed his pyjama top. His ribs were bound tightly with cloth, scented with lilacs. With Seren's 'white witch' tendencies out in the open, she had boldly performed a healing spell on the boy, so that the cracks in his ribs would dissolve. He hadn't complained about pain since.

Gabriel slipped the clean shirt over his head and hurriedly buttoned it. Annabel was sat at the table, grumpily chewing on an apple. She didn't support Gabriel's plans to visit the palace whatsoever. As far as she was concerned, the palace was off limits until Prince Delwyn got up off his backside and apologised to Seren for being so mean.

"If you see him, tell him I'm sorry," Seren confided.

"He knows it," Gabriel promised her.

She leaned against the kitchen counter and followed Gabriel with her eyes as he made his way to her room, to slip his trousers on.

"Men are all pigs anyway," Annabel announced amicably.

"Some more than others I suppose," Seren agreed, thinking of her no-good, rotten ex-husband.

Annabel placed her apple core on the table and swung her legs backwards and forwards in thought. She had been meaning to ask Seren something, but hadn't found the courage to do so, until now.

"Seren?"

"Hmm?" She had begun wiping her counter down with a wet rag, disposing of last nights crumbs in case vermin infested her home.

"You know that song you sang, by the river?"

"The one I wrote about my husband?"

"Yes. That one."

"What of it?"

"Well, it's so cruel. It just doesn't seem...like you."

Seren paused mid-wipe. "A woman isn't always perfect, child. She must have her vices. We all must. And singing is mine."

"Even if it's wicked?"

Seren turned to face her. "I am the child of a black witch. I feel my mother's darkness inside me here." She patted her chest. "She used to call to me on the wind, but I would fight to stay away. You must understand, there is madness in me. But I have learned to tame it. Just as Eli will control his blood lust in time, I should think."

Annabel digested this information and wondered if Seren was dangerous, but when she looked at the woman's bare feet; the tumble of her brown hair and the many skirts; the way she'd cared for her in Gabriel's absence; the fact she was the only person in the kingdom who had offered them a roof over their heads; she realised there was nothing to fear in this woman.

*

Miriam and Elanor were at the gates when Gabriel arrived. Their helmets were shed and their smiles the biggest he'd ever seen.

"All hail Gabriel," Miriam spoke up. "Bringer of peace."

Both bowed to the boy as he passed, timidly smiling back.

The King's maid – Emily – met Gabriel at the door and led him through the palace swiftly.

"They await your arrival," she informed him, when they'd reached the door to the throne room.

Gabriel sucked in a lungful of air. He stuck a finger beneath his collar to stretch it away from his burning neck, then wiped his brow with the back of his hand. Was the palace hot, or was it just him?

When the doors opened, he sensed a massive intake of breath from the people within. The room was filled to bursting, with people of the Kingdom all waiting to see the boy that have lifted the curse at last. Men with stumps patted him on the back, dressed in their finest clothes and women raised hands to their mouthes, whispering to one another.

At the front of the crowd, on a platform, sat the King in all his finery. His gold throne was surrounded by three smaller thrones, two on his left and one on his right. Prince Delwyn, proudly crowned, sat on his father's right. He wore a suit of purple and gold trimmings. His sister's Rosemary and Floriana sat to their father's left, elegantly poised with knees together and hands on their laps, also wearing dresses of purple tones.

They bowed their heads in acknowledgement as Gabriel stood before them, and he in return, got to his knees.

He kept his head down, even though he suffered a burning desire to look at Rosemary. He had only caught a glimpse of her beauty on his passage through the audience. She coyly stared back at him from beneath dark lashes, her hair perfectly coiffed beneath a tiara that caught the light of the torches.

Floriana had been stubbornly averting her gaze all the while, pretending to be more interested in the shine of the marble floors.

The King rose and the whispering stopped. He stepped down from the platform and approached Gabriel. When he was close enough, he lifted his free arm, for the other grasped a walking stick, and wrapped it around Gabriel's back.

A great cheer broke out.

"My boy," the King beamed at him. "A great service you have done for my Kingdom."

The cheers died away as they strained to hear the King's words.

"My son tells me you slayed the witch and lifted the curse and for that I am forever grateful."

Gabriel looked at Delwyn, who inclined his head to the boy.

"Ask of me anything, and I will decide whether it is of reasonable measure, in comparison to your bravery."

Gabriel opened his mouth and closed it. He looked over the King's shoulder at Rosemary, who had moved forward to the edge of her throne as if wanting to be as close to him as possible, without breaking the rules.

"Come on lad, no need to be shy. It has been a great many years since I looked upon my daughter's faces and to see them grown up is a blessing beyond compare. Speak now. What is it you ask of me and I will try my best to grant it."

Gabriel swallowed to clear his throat. "Then...may I be so bold as to ask for your daughter's hand?"

A great gasp erupted and whispering followed.

The King waved his hand to silence them.

At first, he looked annoyed. But his intense gaze melted into that of joy.

"I could not want for a finer man to marry my little girl!" He patted Gabriel on the back once more. "Which one do you ask for?"

Gabriel registered the look of hope in Floriana's

eyes and felt a pang of guilt. He sympathised with the girl, whose heart wasn't even half as pure as her beautiful sisters, and yet the memory of his arms being shredded with a knife led him to forget about her pain. She did not deserve him, even if she asked for his forgiveness.

"Rosemary," he said.

"Do you take this boy, Rosemary?"

"Yes!" she cried, and leapt up.

She jumped from the platform and flung herself at Gabriel, wrapping her hands around his neck and kissing him hard for all to see.

He stared into her blue eyes and felt his heart brimming with light and love. He could not believe it; he had gone from a lonesome vampire with a sad existence to a boy of flesh and blood and a soul full of unimaginable love. He'd found his fairy tale ending, and he'd never even been looking for one.

But the moment was broken when Floriana stood up with a yell of "No!" and fled from the throne room, through a door behind them.

*

She hadn't cried in years. Not since her mother died. But now, she couldn't seem to stop.

The Knights at the gates didn't try to prevent her from passing. They were too alarmed by the running Princess and expected to see people following. But none came.

Floriana made her way along the lane and into the woods, where she kicked at tree stumps with her stupid high heels that the maids had given her to wear. They were difficult to walk in and the heavy gown hindered her stride. When she was ready to turn back, her left heel snapped and she fell to the mossy earth in a heap.

Dismayed and flustered, she stayed there and cried some more into her dirty palms.

"Hello?" came a voice.

She snapped her head up in alarm.

"Are you all right, Miss?"

A boy with copper coloured hair was crouched down on a rock nearby, overlooking her with interest. He looked pale and muscular, beneath a partially unbuttoned shirt.

"I fell, that's all," she explained dismissively.

"You're sad?"

"Yes."

"Why?"

"For many reasons that I will not share with a stranger."

"I'm Elijah," the stranger said. "But people call me Eli."

She turned away from him, picking up a stick and poking it into the earth. "Floriana."

"That's a pretty name."

She rolled her eyes. "You don't have to lie because my father is the King."

"Your father is the King? So that would make you a Princess?"

She nodded and looked over her shoulder at him with a frown. "You're not from around here are you?"

He shook his head. "No. But I like it here. The

woods are great for hunting."

"You hunt?" She felt her spirits lift.

Eli pulled his face back into the shadows to conceal his fangs from her eager sight.

"Sometimes."

"Me too," she replied. "I love it, but my sister thinks I'm evil for it."

"People need to hunt to eat, right?"

She tried standing up. She wanted to see the boy better. It was dark in the woods because the sunlight struggled to breech the canopy overhead. Unsteadily, she rose and the moment she took a step forward, her ankle gave way in a burst of pain.

Eli reacted in the blink of an eye, catching the Princess before she fell. She looked up into his face and saw the fangs protruding from his gums. She reached up and touched one with her fingertip.

"So strange," she said.

He looked away, embarrassed. "I'm sorry."

"No. It's all right. I've just never seen such fangs."

"I won't hurt you," he promised. "Here, let me take you home. Climb on my back."

She was sceptical of this offer, until the boys arms made light work of gripping her legs and carrying her away.

"You're so strong."

"Maybe you're just light," he suggested.

"Eli?"

"Yes?"

"Would you like to stay for tea?"

Eli's pace was inhuman, but the Princess said nothing. She relished the wind in her hair and the grip of his hands on her thighs, pinning her body safely to his back as he moved.

"Princess, I don't think that would be wise."

"Why not?"

"Because I'm...I'm a vampire."

He didn't know it, but she smiled into the strands of his copper coloured hair.

"That's all right," she whispered mischievously into his ear. "Just stay and chat then."

"I'd like that," he said.

*

Seren paced her hut. Gabriel would not be returning, and she'd made peace with that. But now she was alone.

"You've been alone before," she encouraged herself quietly. "You've been alone for years at a time. Don't be silly."

She wiped her nose with a rag and walked to her bedroom, but as she reached the doorway, there came a knock.

"Who is it?" she called.

"Delwyn."

Her heart somersaulted as he pushed open the door.

"My Prince," she curtsied respectfully, but her heart wasn't entirely in it.

He raised a hand to stop her. "Don't. You don't have to do that around me."

She placed her hands in front of her and chewed the skin inside her mouth, waiting anxiously for him to state why he'd come. She had nothing more to say to him; nothing that could break the spell of silence that had shrouded them for days now.

"I thought you'd come to the palace today."

"I didn't think I had a right to. I let the Kingdom down."

He sighed. "Look, I understand why you protected her."

"Oh really?" she snorted.

He took a step towards her.

She folded her arms over her chest.

"Love makes people crazy."

"So I'm crazy now, am I?"

He was close enough to touch her.

"You were right. She was your mother –"

"Yes, and now she's gone and you have your sisters back."

"To which I am indebted to you." Finally, he took her hand in his. Her skin was cold and her arms goose-pimpled. He lifted her hand to his lips and kissed the tops of her knuckles gently.

"Forgive me," he whispered.

She tried to maintain a look of cold indifference, until her lips cracked into a smile.

"You are forgiven."

"Good, now come with me to the palace. Grey-shadow is outside, we can ride."

"What's wrong with my hut?" she teased.

Delwyn scooped her up off the floor and she cried

out in delight.

"How can I make you Queen, if you stay here?" he asked her, and kissed her on the tip of her nose.

*

As a further gift bestowed upon Gabriel by the King, he was knighted before the court. Prince Delwyn performed the ceremony, for his father's legs had weakened and he could not easily leave his throne.

The crowds celebrated for days. The streets of the Black Kingdom were filled with dancing and laughter, singing and merriment. And all those men who had lost their hands forgot their troubles in the light of a new era.

Gabriel and Rosemary married in the spring, moving to a summer palace a day's ride away. Between mountains, a valley opened up and the land became theirs to watch over.

Annabel came with them, having grown attached (in time) to the Princess. They brushed each other's hair and adorned themselves with flowers from their garden. They chased their puppies around the fields and splashed about in the river that ran through the valley, clear blue and absent of severed hands.

Gabriel was a proud husband. He ploughed fields on days when the sunshine was bright and read Annabel books on the days that rain pummelled the earth. He was a fine Prince to his people that followed him and was not afraid of hard work, much to everyone's happiness.

Rosemary could not have married a finer man, and she told him this every day.

Finally, he'd found a place in the world.
Finally, he had a home.

About the Author

Karla has a First Class Honour in Creative and
Professional Writing

She has 26 tattoos, most of which are literature based and
likes to model as a hobby.

She lives in Cardiff Bay and hopes to win the lottery very
soon so she can feed her ball gown desires.